D1024118

Elizabeth Gail and the Silent Piano

Hilda Stahl

Tyndale House Publishers, Inc., Wheaton, Illinois

Dedicated with love to
Gene, Sandy, Bracey, Neal, Debbie
and Shelly Clements

The Elizabeth Gail Series

1 *Elizabeth Gail and the Mystery at the Johnson Farm*
2 *Elizabeth Gail and the Secret Box*
3 *Elizabeth Gail and the Teddy Bear Mystery*
4 *Elizabeth Gail and the Dangerous Double*
5 *Elizabeth Gail and Trouble at Sandhill Ranch*
6 *Elizabeth Gail and the Strange Birthday Party*
7 *Elizabeth Gail and the Terrifying News*
8 *Elizabeth Gail and the Frightened Runaways*
9 *Elizabeth Gail and Trouble from the Past*
10 *Elizabeth Gail and the Silent Piano*
11 *Elizabeth Gail and Double Trouble*
12 *Elizabeth Gail and the Holiday Mystery*
13 *Elizabeth Gail and the Missing Love Letters*
14 *Elizabeth Gail and the Music Camp Romance*
15 *Elizabeth Gail and the Handsome Stranger*
16 *Elizabeth Gail and the Secret Love*
17 *Elizabeth Gail and the Summer for Weddings*
18 *Elizabeth Gail and the Time for Love*

Cover and interior illustrations by Kathy Kulin

Juvenile trade paper edition

Library of Congress Catalog Card Number 88-51707
ISBN 0-8423-0810-5

Printed in the United States of America

2 3 4 5 6 7 8 9 10 95 94 93 92 91 90

Contents

ONE
A failure

Libby closed her bedroom door as carefully as she could. Her legs gave way and she slumped to the floor, her back against the door, her pointed chin pressed against her thin chest. Hot tears slipped down her pale cheeks. Oh, what a failure she was! And this was to have been *her* day.

She pulled her knees up and smoothed the soft lavender dress down her legs. How beautiful she had felt just a few hours ago. But *nothing* could change ugly Elizabeth Gail Dobbs into beautiful Elizabeth Gail Johnson, concert pianist, loved daughter of Chuck and Vera Johnson.

Libby pressed her hands against her eyes and moaned. How the Johnson family must be laughing at her!

Libby stiffened, her head up, as she heard Kevin and Toby outside in the hallway. She didn't want them coming in to talk to her. She didn't want any of the Johnsons to see her now.

She sagged in relief as the boys moved on and she

heard a door slam down the hall. Were they laughing at her? Was Toby acting proud of himself because he was already adopted into the Johnson family and she wasn't? Maybe Kevin and Ben and Susan were thankful that she wasn't their real sister yet.

Libby pressed her face against her knees and closed her eyes tightly. Grandma and Grandpa Johnson were probably sitting in the family room this minute chuckling and joking about Elizabeth Gail Dobbs, *failure*.

Libby sighed as she awkwardly pushed herself up and walked to her bed. She flopped onto her stomach and buried her face against Pinky's fur. Just a few hours ago she'd dressed in her long lavender dress and been proud and sure of herself. She could play Beethoven's *Für Elise* without any mistakes. It was in her memory and her heart—a complete part of her. The tiny twinge of butterflies beforehand didn't bother her.

Libby squeezed Pinky tighter. She could see herself walking confidently to the piano, a beautiful baby grand similar to the one that she played at Rachael Avery's house. Before she sat down she looked back at the large audience. The smile had frozen on her face and her arms and legs had refused to cooperate. She'd sat down awkwardly, then just sat there. Beethoven's *Für Elise* had completely left her mind. And her music was at home on Vera's piano. Why had Rachael Avery insisted that she come without music?

Libby had touched the high E, then struck it again. What came next? Then she remembered. She struck D sharp, then back to E, D sharp again, then E. Finally she came in with the bass notes and for a while she knew it was going smoothly. Suddenly her fingers refused to move. Perspiration dotted her face and her dress felt too hot. She could tell that her carefully curled hair was down to its usual brown straggle.

Why had she thought she could be a concert pianist? Why had she taken piano lessons from the famous Rachael Avery?

Finally Libby had stumbled through her music and walked stiff-legged back to sit with her family. The clapping had sounded hollow to her ears. She could smell Vera's perfume as she patted Libby on the leg.

The floor should've opened up and swallowed her. And how could Rachael Avery stand in front of everyone and say that she was proud of her students? Even when Rachael had sat at the piano and played, Libby could not enjoy it.

And in the car coming home everyone had said what a fine job their Elizabeth had done. She had wanted to open the station wagon door and get out right in the middle of a busy street. She had forced herself to sit still with her hands folded in her lap.

Libby sat up on her bed and hugged Pinky close. Tears stung her eyes. How could she face the Johnson family? They knew she was a failure at piano, especially Vera who played so beautifully. Libby nodded sadly. They were being nice to her because she was a poor foster kid who had tried to get too big for her own good. She was an aid kid, nothing more. Aid kids couldn't expect to become famous concert pianists or famous anything else!

Libby looked around her pink, dark pink, and red bedroom. An aid kid didn't deserve a bedroom this beautiful either. She should live in a run-down, shabby apartment with a mother who beat her and starved her and deserted her. She didn't deserve to live on a big farm in the beautiful Johnson home!

"I'll never play the piano again," muttered Libby. "I hate piano! I hate music!"

She spotted the tiny grand piano sitting proudly on her dresser. Slowly she walked over and picked it up, remembering the day last spring when Joe Wilkens had given it to her. She'd been very happy and proud of it. Joe had wanted her to have a gift because Toby Smart was now Toby Johnson and everyone had brought him gifts and said nice things to him to celebrate his adoption. And she had been only Libby Dobbs, aid kid.

"I hate you, piano," she whispered fiercely. She lifted it high to throw it across the room, then lowered her arm. She could not break the piano that Joe had given her. She would keep it forever! Every time she looked at it, she would think of Joe. But she'd force herself to forget her big dream of being a concert pianist. Then she'd have more time to spend with Joe.

"Please, Libby, come play Monopoly with me," Joe had said often the past few weeks.

"I can't, Joe. I have to practice piano."

"Ben won't play. He and Adam are always playing chess and they don't want me around."

Libby had felt bad for Joe. "Go play with Susan. She's good at Monopoly. And she likes Clue and Ping-Pong."

So, Joe had played with Susan. But now Joe wouldn't have to settle for Susan. Libby smiled tightly. Now she'd have all the time she wanted to play with Joe.

Libby set the tiny grand piano on her dresser, then picked it up and pushed it to the back of her underwear drawer. Someday she'd get it out and set it back on top of the dresser—someday when she wouldn't cry at the sight of it.

"No more piano lessons! No more practice!"

Libby stopped, her head up, her hazel eyes wide. Now, Joanne Tripper would take piano from Rachael Avery. Libby's stomach tightened and she shook her head. A picture of snooty, blonde-haired Joanne Tripper flashed in Libby's mind.

"You don't look like a concert pianist, Libby," Joanne had said often. "You look like a poor aid kid pretending to dream a big dream. *I* will be the famous concert pianist. I will take from Rachael Avery and you won't! She'll soon know that I'm better than you."

Libby's thin chest rose and fell. Now that she wasn't going to take piano lessons, Rachael would have room for a new student and that student would be Joanne Tripper.

"So, who cares?" Libby gritted her teeth and closed her eyes. She didn't care! She had no reason to care. She was never going to play the piano again.

TWO
A long walk

Libby walked cautiously down the stairs, her hand on the shiny rail. It was barely light outside and she knew everyone was still asleep. Toby's loud snores followed Libby down the stairs. The grandfather clock ticked loudly and Libby noticed that it was almost seven-thirty. Chuck would be getting up soon to go to his store in town. Everyone had to get up to do the chores, but on Saturday they slept in until eight. She'd be back from her walk by then. No one would even notice that she was gone. Maybe they wouldn't care anyway.

Rex barked and ran to her side as she zipped her jacket against the chilly wind. She flipped her hood up with one hand and patted Rex with the other.

"Want to go for a walk with me, Rex?" Her voice seemed to echo in the quiet farmyard.

Slowly she walked down the long driveway toward the paved road. It was too wet to walk back in the pasture and trees. The large trees in the front yard were bare except for the one with the heavy rope swing hanging from it. The grass under the swing was almost worn away and bare dirt showed.

Rachael had cancelled today's lessons because of last night's recital. Libby frowned and pushed the thought away. She would not think about piano. She would enjoy the brisk chilly day with Rex at her side.

She stopped at the end of the driveway and remembered the day she'd come to the Johnson farm a year ago. Miss Miller had brought her out and a big white goose had attacked her. Libby grinned. Goosy Poosy was almost her friend now but at the time she'd been scared beyond words. Then she'd met the family and looked at the horses and her new bedroom all to herself and she panicked. She hadn't wanted to stay long enough to fall in love with the place only to be kicked out again. So, she'd taken her shabby suitcase and sneaked out of the house. But Chuck Johnson had found her and talked her into staying.

Maybe now he was sorry. But he said they'd prayed her into the family.

"I won't think about it!" She looked down at Rex and he was looking up at her. "Let's walk, Rex."

Libby looked toward the big white colonial house where the Wilkens lived. Would Joe be up yet? Later today she'd invite him over to go horseback riding.

Libby looked in the other direction where Grandma Feuder lived, the woman who was "grandma" to everyone in name only. Except Adam. She was Adam's real great-grandma and he lived with her, along with his parents when they were around. But they were in New Guinea for the winter, so Adam and Grandma Feuder were alone.

Slowly Libby walked down the quiet road. Two cars

and a pickup drove past, going toward town. Libby was glad that Rex wasn't like some dogs she'd seen who chased cars. Rex stayed close beside her and ignored the cars.

At Grandma Feuder's place a dog barked and Libby thought it sounded like Lapdog. Rex turned his head but didn't bark. Libby wondered if Grandma was sitting at her kitchen table with a mug of hot tea. Or maybe she was still in bed, covered with the quilt that she'd made when she was first a bride.

Birds chirped in the bushes along the road. Cattails stood up tall and brown in the watery ditches. Toby and Kevin often came here to catch frogs and turtles.

Rex growled low in his throat and Libby stopped, her heart racing. She looked around but couldn't see anything or anyone.

"What is it, Rex?" she whispered, looking anxiously around. She looked toward the ditch where it was quite shallow, then gasped as she clutched Rex's collar. She swallowed hard and walked slowly toward what looked like a dead body lying in the ditch. Or maybe someone had tossed out a bundle of clothes. No, it was a body!

"Oh, Rex," she said in a low frantic voice. "What shall we do?" Her hands trembled and her legs felt as if they couldn't support her another minute.

Should she run to get Adam or call the police? Her heart felt as if it would leap out of her sweatshirt and through her jacket.

Slowly she forced herself to walk alongside of the road until she could see the body better. Rex pulled free and walked into the ditch. Libby stood with her hand over her mouth, holding back a scream. Rex stuck his nose against the exposed cheek, then barked.

Suddenly the body moved, then jumped up in alarm.

Libby almost fainted in relief. It was a girl, a little older than she was and a lot bigger. As she walked out of the ditch, Libby had to look up at her. The girl was at least a head taller and about seventy-five pounds heavier.

"Hi," she said with a wide grin. She pulled a weed out of her short brown hair. "Did I scare you?"

"A little." Libby cleared her throat. "Well, maybe a lot."

"Sorry. I'm writing a book."

"Writing a book?"

The girl nodded. "I was 'experiencing.' I needed to know how it felt to be knocked out and lying face down in a ditch." She lifted a plump shoulder. "So, I came out here and tried it."

"Sorry we bothered you."

"That's all right. I was done." She frowned thoughtfully. "I'd say it felt cold and uncomfortable, but at least this time of year there are no bugs or snakes. I'll have to keep that in mind. I might want insects just to bring in sounds." She stuck her hands in her jacket pockets. "You know how important it is to get the senses involved."

Libby frowned. She didn't know what the girl was talking about. "I guess Rex and I had better go home."

"Wait." The girl studied Libby with her eyes narrowed. "Tell me how it feels to be short and thin."

"I'm tall. I'm always taller than everyone else."

The girl shook her head. "Look at me. I'm tall! I'm five feet eight and thirteen years old."

"I'm five-four and twelve years old. Maybe when I'm

thirteen I'll be as tall as you are." Libby couldn't imagine being that big at once.

"You wouldn't want to be this big." She rolled her eyes. "Boys won't have anything to do with me. I'm too big and I guess I scare them and make them feel inferior." She shrugged and made a face. "Who needs boys? Not me! I'm going to be a famous writer by the time I'm sixteen."

A sharp pain stabbed Libby's heart. Just two days ago she would have said she was going to be a famous concert pianist, but not now. "I never tried to write a book," was all she could say.

"Don't feel bad about that. I don't know anyone else my age who has. I'm sure there are others like me out there, but I haven't met them yet. I like to keep to myself. I have more time to think that way."

"I guess I'd better go." Libby turned toward home, Rex close beside her.

"I'm Jill."

Libby turned back. "I'm Libby." She didn't tell Jill that several people call her Elizabeth. She felt dull and drab and worthless.

Jill held her hand out, a soft expression on her face. "Why are you sad, Libby?"

She ducked her head to hide the sudden tears. "I've got to go."

"I didn't mean to make you cry. I guess I'm too curious about feelings and things. Sorry."

"That's all right."

"I'd better go, too, or my folks will think I've been kidnapped. Although I don't think anybody would fool with me." Jill chuckled and shrugged. "Only a mother could want me. And a dad."

Libby twisted her toe in the dirt beside the road. Mother didn't want her. And Dad had deserted her when she was only three.

"Hey, do you play the piano?" asked Jill excitedly.

Libby's head snapped up. "Why?"

"One of the characters in my book plays the piano and I need to know a few things to make it authentic." She scratched her head. "Do you play?"

"No! Not anymore." Libby turned to leave but Jill caught her arm.

"What do you mean? Why not anymore?"

Libby's face burned and she knew her cheeks were bright red. "I don't want to talk about it!"

"Why are you mad?" Jill's grip tightened on Libby's arm.

"Leave me alone!" Libby jerked free, her eyes flashing. "Mind your own business!" She turned toward home and ran along the road, her tennis shoes slapping the pavement. She heard Jill shout at her but she kept running with Rex beside her. Maybe she'd run forever so that she wouldn't have to think about piano or anything else.

THREE
Grandma Feuder's new neighbors

Libby folded her arms and leaned back in Chuck's big chair. She tried to keep her eyes on Saturday morning cartoons, but they kept straying to the piano sitting silently against the wall.

A fire crackled in the fireplace. Kevin, Toby, Ben, and Susan sat watching cartoons and occasionally laughing. Libby couldn't see anything funny. Tears stung her eyes, not from cartoons but from the empty feeling she had when she looked at the piano.

Usually she'd be on her way to town with Vera to take lessons from Rachael Avery. Libby was glad she didn't have to face Rachael today. After last night's recital, Rachael might not want "Libby the Failure" as a student. Libby twisted a piece of brown hair around and around her finger. Joanne Tripper probably *was* a better pianist. *She* wouldn't freeze up in front of an audience.

Libby twisted in agitation. Oh, she couldn't sit still another minute! She jumped up.

"What's wrong, Libby?" asked Susan, looking around

at Libby. Susan was lying on her stomach on the thick carpet with her elbows on the floor and her hands propping up her head. Her red-gold hair was in two long braids, one over each slender shoulder.

"Cartoons are boring," cried Libby.

"Quiet!" Toby looked around with a frown, then back at the TV.

"If you don't want to watch, then get out of here," said Kevin, punching his glasses against his round face.

"Gladly!" Libby rushed from the room, then stopped just outside the door. She didn't want to go to her room where she'd have too much time to think, and she didn't want to tell Vera she didn't have anything to do or Vera would find some chore to give her.

"I'll visit Grandma Feuder," she said under her breath in satisfaction. Where was Vera? "Mom!"

"I'm in the study, Elizabeth."

Libby smiled. Vera tried very hard to call her Elizabeth instead of Libby. Vera knew she liked it better.

Vera sat behind Chuck's big oak desk, writing in the ledger book. She looked up and smiled. "What can I do for you, honey?"

"Is it all right if I go visit Grandma Feuder for a while right now? I have my room cleaned and the chores done." Libby stood quietly as Vera frowned thoughtfully. Vera looked pretty with her blonde hair curled softly around her face. She had the same blue eyes as Kevin and Susan.

"Call Grandma and if it's all right with her, then you can visit for a while. If she needs help with anything, then give her a hand."

"I will, Mom." Libby turned to go but Vera spoke to her and she reluctantly turned back.

"You did fine last night, Elizabeth, considering it was your first performance in front of an audience." Vera smiled and Libby turned and walked out without saying anything.

She stopped in the kitchen and leaned against the counter, her heart racing. How could Vera say she'd done fine? Why didn't she tell the truth and tell her that she'd never succeed at anything, especially at being a concert pianist?

Finally Libby dialed Grandma Feuder and gained permission to visit. Grandma seemed excited, and Libby hoped Grandma wouldn't comment on the recital.

Several minutes later Libby stood her bike beside Grandma's porch and walked to the door of the old farmhouse. Dogs barked inside as she knocked, and Libby smiled. All of Grandma's dogs knew her now and liked her.

Adam opened the door and stood aside as Libby walked into the warm house that smelled like cinnamon rolls.

"What's Ben doing?" asked Adam as he closed the door.

Libby wrinkled her small straight nose and pulled off her jacket. "He's glued to the TV watching cartoons."

"I'm going over to play chess with him."

"Again?" Libby felt disappointed. She'd wanted to talk with Adam as well as Grandma. "You and Ben haven't stopped playing chess for days."

"We're having a tournament and so far he's winning."

Adam's brown eyes sparkled and he scratched his head. "But I've been studying his moves and I think I can beat him."

Libby shrugged. What was so great about chess? Ben had tried to teach her but she hadn't had the time or patience to learn, not with piano practice.

"Hello, Elizabeth." Grandma wiped her hands on her apron as she walked to Libby, then hugged her warmly. "It's good to see you. My, you smell like fresh outdoors. You look pretty today with your cheeks pink and all."

Libby flushed and looked down at her feet. She knew she was tall and thin and ugly. How could Grandma say she was pretty?

"I'm going to take a few things to my new neighbors. I thought you might enjoy going with me." Grandma patted Libby's arm and smiled.

Libby's stomach tightened in a knot. It was still hard for her to meet new people. They always wanted to know why her name was different from the others in her family.

"Since Libby's going with you, Grandma, she can help you carry the things," said Adam. "I'll go to Ben's right now and play chess." Adam grabbed his jacket and left before Libby could say that she didn't want to go with Grandma.

"How about a cup of cocoa, Elizabeth?" Grandma walked to the stove and turned the fire on under a pot. "I'll just heat it up a little and it'll be ready. I'll give you a cinnamon roll to go with it."

Libby sat at the table and reached down to pat Lapdog on the head. She'd rather have a cup of cocoa and a cinnamon roll than go visit people she didn't know.

Grandma set the cup of steaming cocoa in front of Libby, then made herself a cup of tea. She sat down and smoothed her flowered apron. Her white hair was combed in neat waves around her head. She smiled and the wrinkles around her eyes deepened. "I'm going to be your Sunday school teacher tomorrow. Connie Tol is on vacation and won't be back until next Saturday."

Libby smiled. "I like to hear you tell Bible stories."

"I like to tell them. I like to share what Jesus has done for me, too." She sipped her tea, then set the tan mug down. "I wonder if the new family goes to church anywhere. I think I'll invite them to ours."

Libby sat very still, her hands around the mug of cocoa. Could she invite people, strangers at that, to come to church? Maybe she should go home and let Grandma go alone. But she couldn't do that. Grandma needed help carrying things to them.

"I'm taking some winter squash, cinnamon rolls, and a couple dozen eggs to my neighbors." Grandma picked up a silver spoon and stirred her tea. "Ted and Freida Noteboom and two children. I don't know how old the children are. I'll enjoy having neighbors again after the house being empty for so long."

Libby didn't want to talk about the new neighbors, but she listened to Grandma patiently, nodding now and then.

Later Libby walked beside Grandma down the side of the road past the place where she'd met Jill earlier. Libby looked around but the girl was gone, maybe off "experiencing" somewhere else.

"What a pretty mailbox," said Grandma, laughing. "I like the bright colors on it. And it's large. Must get a lot of mail."

Libby thought the mailbox was strange-looking and as she looked toward the house she wondered who had painted it that way. Maybe she'd meet some very weird people today. The house was an ordinary two-story white farmhouse.

The door burst open before they could knock. "Hi! Are you Mrs. Feuder? I'm Paul Noteboom. Mom said to tell you to come right in." The boy held the door wide. To Libby, he looked about Kevin's age and size. His eyes and hair were brown and he was dressed in jeans and a blue sweatshirt.

Inside the door Libby looked around in surprise. The large room was a kitchen, dining room, and family room combined and the walls were painted white. Bright splashes of color were at the windows and in the furniture. An open stairway led to another floor above. The TV was on and cartoons were loudly blaring out. Paul dashed over and punched the off button.

"Mom!" he shouted. "Mrs. Feuder is here with a girl."

A door opened next to the large refrigerator and a tall, brown-haired woman walked in, smiling happily. "I'm Freida Noteboom. I'm glad to meet you. I'll call my husband. He wants to get to know you, too." She turned to Paul. "Go get Dad, but please don't shout for him."

Paul ran off and Freida Noteboom invited Libby and Grandma to have a seat. Grandma handed over her gifts and the woman thanked her enthusiastically.

"We love it out here in the country after living in town for all our married life. I'd like to get a few chickens and plant a garden in the spring and do a lot of other things that we couldn't do in the city."

A tall, rumpled looking man walked in with Paul beside him. He pulled off his glasses as Freida introduced them around, suddenly realizing that she didn't know Libby. Libby wanted to sink out of sight under the blue flowered couch, but she managed a smile when Grandma introduced her.

Ted Noteboom sat on a straight-backed chair and crossed his legs. He pushed his fingers through his brown hair. "I was trying to find a way to get out of my study. I'm thankful for this kind visit." He smiled at Grandma. "I like the look of your place. Your barn must have been built over a hundred years ago."

Libby listened with one ear while she looked around, wondering where the second child was. Kevin and Toby would be glad to meet Paul.

A door slammed and Ted looked over his shoulder. "That must be our long lost girl. Yes, it is."

Libby gasped. It was Jill, the girl she'd met in the ditch.

"Hi, Libby," she said with a wide smile.

Libby swallowed hard. "Hi, Jill."

FOUR
Stolen kiss

Libby reluctantly followed Jill Noteboom up the wide stairs. After Grandma Feuder and Jill's parents had gotten over the surprise that the girls knew each other, Jill had asked if she and Libby could go upstairs. Libby had wanted to run out the front door and back home. She would have, too, but she hadn't wanted to embarrass Grandma Feuder.

"Here's my room," said Jill proudly as she pushed a heavy door wide. "I have an electric typewriter of my own. Dad knows how important one is to a writer." Jill smiled and Libby wondered how this stranger could be so talkative. "What's wrong, Libby? Are you still mad at me?"

Libby sank down on a small couch in the corner of the bedroom. "I never met anyone like you before."

Jill shrugged. "I know." She sat on the corner of her desk and crossed her ankles. "I can't bother with acting like a normal thirteen-year-old. I want to make it by the time I'm sixteen, so I don't have any time to waste. I need to learn what makes people respond the way they do. Dad is forty years old and he just made it two years ago."

Libby frowned. "Made it?" What did this strange girl mean?

"He is successful now," Jill said smugly.

"What does he do?"

Jill jumped to her feet, her hands out. "What does he do? Don't you *know?* He's Ted Noteboom."

Libby frowned and squirmed in agitation. She had to get away from this girl. Why hadn't she stayed home this morning? Watching cartoons would've been better than this!

Jill's eyes narrowed and she stood with her hands on her hips. "I can see you've never heard of Ted Noteboom, the author of the famous Vern Steel Series. Where have you been the past two years? Everybody, *everybody* reads his books!"

"I haven't." Libby lifted her pointed chin defiantly. "And I don't think anyone else has either!"

"Oh? Why do you say that? Not everyone can be as ignorant as you!"

Libby pushed herself up, her hazel eyes flashing. "You don't know anything, Jill Noteboom! I don't have time to read. I am going to be a famous concert pianist and *that* takes a lot of practice!"

"A concert pianist! Fantastic!" Jill grabbed her notebook, flipped it open, and held her pencil poised over it. "How does it feel? Is this a burning desire?"

Libby's stomach cramped and her legs gave way. She dropped on the couch and covered her burning face with icy hands. Suddenly she felt Jill sit down beside her and pat her knee.

"Don't be upset, Libby. I don't know what's wrong,

but I'm sorry I hurt you. Can you tell me what's wrong?"

Libby shook her head, her brain whirling with ways to get away from Jill, away from this house, without making Grandma feel badly.

"Here, Libby. Take this."

Libby felt the soft tissue against her hand and she took it and blew her nose and wiped away the tears that had escaped even though she'd tried to keep them back. "I have to go home," she whispered.

"All right. I'll walk you downstairs."

"I don't want anyone to see me."

"We'll go down the back stairs and Paul and I will walk Grandma Feuder home when she's done visiting."

Libby looked up at Jill thankfully. "Don't tell her what happened."

Jill patted Libby's thin shoulder. "I won't. I'll just say that you had to get right home."

She smile hesitantly. "Will you be all right?"

Libby nodded, wondering if she would be.

"Come on." Jill led the way and Libby followed, glad that Jill had gotten her jacket for her. "Bye, Libby. I'll see you Monday on the bus."

Libby took a deep breath. "Grandma's going to ask if all of you can come to our church tomorrow."

Jill grinned and nodded her brown bangs almost touching her dark brows. "We'll be there. We're Christians, too. I heard Dad and Grandma when I got your jacket, and I know we're going to your church."

"Then I'll see you tomorrow." Libby started to walk away, then stopped and turned. "I'll save a chair beside me in Sunday school class for you."

"Thanks, Libby." She crossed her arms over her

plump body and hunched her shoulders against the cold. "Do you think we could be friends? I think we'd have fun together. I hope you don't waste your time with boys yet."

Libby thought of Joe Wilkens. She really hadn't had time to waste on boys or anything else. "I don't."

"Good, then we can be friends. I won't have time for a boyfriend until I'm at least twenty. Then when I'm twenty-seven I want to get married and have two children, both boys."

Libby turned to go, tears filling her eyes. She had had her future planned until last night's disaster. Now, what would she do with her life? Maybe Chuck would let her be a clerk in his general store when she was old enough. Cold wind blew against her and she flipped up her hood and tied it in place.

What would she do with all her free time now? What would Rachael Avery say when she told her she was dropping piano? How would Chuck and Vera react?

Libby walked tiredly to Grandma's house, got her bike, and rode toward home, her mind busy with thoughts for the future, for the next minute. Already her fingers itched to touch the piano keys again. But that couldn't be! She didn't want to play. The piano would be silent from now on except when Vera played. Libby turned into the long drive. From now on the only piano she would touch would be the tiny grand piano that Joe had given her.

Joe's bike stood beside the house and Libby smiled. Joe was here to see her. He'd be glad that she didn't have piano today.

Libby started for the back door, then stopped at a sound in the horse barn. The door was open and someone was inside. Maybe Susan was helping Joe saddle up so they could go riding.

With a happy smile Libby ran toward the barn. Goosy Poosy honked from inside the chicken pen and Rex barked from his doghouse where someone had tied him up. Libby stood just in the door of the barn, her mouth open ready to call out to Joe or Susan or whoever was in the barn. Joe and Susan stood outside Apache Girl's stall with their arms around each other, kissing.

Libby groaned and they jumped apart, flushed with embarrassment.

"Libby," whispered Susan, rubbing the back of her hand over her mouth.

"Hi, Libby," said Joe. "I came over to go riding with Susan."

"Oh," said Libby in a small voice. She turned and Susan called her name but she couldn't turn back.

"Do you want to go with us?"

"No," said Libby.

"You've got to practice piano anyway," said Joe sharply. "You always do."

Libby spun around, her eyes blazing, her fists knotted at her sides. "But not today, Joe, and not ever again! You and Susan go riding and have fun!"

"Why are you mad?" asked Joe impatiently. "I like Susan and she likes me. You don't have to get mad about that."

"And don't tell Mom that I kissed Joe," snapped Susan.

"Don't worry! I won't tell anyone! Who wants to know anyway? So what if you kiss Joe all day long? Who cares?" Libby turned and ran to the house, slamming the back door with a bang. She leaned against it, her body shaking. How could Joe kiss Susan? He'd said he liked her! Libby pressed her hands against her cheeks. She'd thought he liked her, not Susan. Joe had given *her* the piano. But maybe he gave Susan something and Susan didn't tell anyone.

Was that the first time Joe had kissed Susan? Maybe he had always liked Susan best but just didn't tell. Libby moaned. Maybe he had only felt sorry for her since she was an aid kid and his sister had been mean to her.

Slowly, with stiff fingers, Libby untied her hood, unzipped her jacket, and pulled it off. Just as she hung it up Vera walked up to her.

"Libby, have you seen. . . ." Vera's voice trailed away and she lifted Libby's chin. "What's wrong, honey?"

Libby pulled away from Vera. "I hate it here!"

"Why?" Vera moved until she was facing Libby. She stood just a little taller than Libby.

"I hate Susan!" Libby pushed past Vera, then looked over her shoulder. "And I hate piano!"

Before she could move, Vera caught her arm. "Let's go talk in the study, Elizabeth."

"I don't want to." She tried to tug free but Vera's grip tightened.

"We're going to talk. You're upset about something and I want to know what it is."

Libby wanted to run from the study and lock herself in her room. She should not have said she hated anything. When would she learn to keep her mouth shut?

"All right, Elizabeth." Vera stood in front of Libby and studied her intently. "Something has been bothering you since last night. I want to know what it is."

Libby locked her fingers together. She couldn't say how she felt about being a failure at piano yet. It would hurt too much.

"Well, Elizabeth?" Right now Vera sounded a lot like Chuck and Libby knew she'd have to say something.

"Joe doesn't like me anymore. He . . . he likes Susan."

Vera pulled Libby close and patted her back. "I'm sorry, honey. I talked to Susan this morning. She was feeling bad because she loves Joe. She doesn't want to hurt you, honey, but she and Joe have been together a lot lately and they really think they're in love."

Libby shivered and pressed her face against Vera's neck. She smelled like roses.

"Growing up isn't always easy, honey, but you have God with you to help you. He can take away the pain you're feeling right now."

"I hate boys!"

"No, you don't. Before long you'll have boys falling for you. Then you'll have to chase them away so you'll have time to practice piano."

Libby stiffened. She would never touch the piano again! Never! She carefully pulled away from Vera. "I'm going to my room."

"Smile, honey. Joe's not the only boy around. What about Adam?"

Libby pushed her hair back and sniffed back a tear. "Ben and Adam are always playing chess. Adam isn't interested in me at all."

"You don't have time for boys anyway. Piano is your life and your dream right now." Vera tugged Libby's hair. "You have a lot of years ahead of you to think about boys. Don't grow up too fast, honey. I told Susan the same thing but she wants so badly to go with a boy that she didn't want to hear what I said." Vera walked with Libby toward the study door. Vera stopped and rested her hands on Libby's shoulders. "Your heavenly Father loves you even more than I do. Allow him to take away your pain."

"I don't know how," said Libby in a low, tight voice.

"It takes forgiving Susan. And Joe."

Libby barely nodded. Oh, she couldn't forgive Susan! Or Joe! No, she could not! She would not!

In her room Libby hurried to her dresser drawer. She would take the tiny grand piano that Joe had given her and she would smash it into a million tiny pieces!

Frantically she searched through her drawer. The piano was gone! She dumped out her drawer and looked again. It *was* gone!

"Susan took it," Libby whispered fiercely. "She doesn't want me to have anything from Joe."

With her eyes flashing and her head high Libby marched to Susan's room. The white and yellow room was in neat order except for a pair of jeans lying on the floor next to the curved leg of Susan's desk. Libby looked around quickly. She couldn't see the piano. Susan probably had hid it, or even broken it and tossed it away.

Slowly Libby walked to a tall chest where Susan kept her favorite things. Libby picked up a china figurine, a blonde child with a gold kitten. Libby's heart raced and her mouth felt cotton-dry.

"She asked for this," whispered Libby fiercely as she struck the girl against the edge of the chest. The breaking sound made Libby's stomach sick.

Libby dropped the pieces of the figurine on the chest and slowly walked into the hall.

"That's what you get for taking my piano, Susan!"

Libby walked slowly to her bedroom and closed the door quietly, then her legs gave way and she sank down on the round, red hassock, trembling and breathing raggedly.

FIVE
Jill's book

Libby's stomach tightened sickeningly as she slipped her long nightgown over her head. It had been hard to sit at the table and eat supper with Susan beside her. Soon Susan would see the broken girl and know who had broken it.

Libby shivered even though her bedroom was toasty warm on such a chilly night. She wouldn't think about Susan or the broken figurine. She would think about helping Ben with his Christmas tree business after Thanksgiving. When would it snow? Maybe tonight.

When would Susan come storming into her bedroom and scream at her for breaking the girl and kitten?

Nervously Libby pleated the soft skirt of her nightgown, her eyes glued to the bedroom door. Soon it would burst open and Susan would rush in, her red-gold hair swirling around her slender shoulders, her blue eyes on fire with anger. Libby leaped up. She dare not just sit still and wait or Susan would know that she'd broken the girl.

Libby reached for her Bible, then jerked her hand

back. How could she read the Bible after what she'd done? She hung her head and closed her eyes. Would she ever be as good as the Johnsons?

Sudenly the door burst open and Susan rushed in, the broken figurine in her open hands. "You did this, Libby! I know you did!"

Libby shrugged. "Who says so?"

"I do!" Susan pushed her face close to Libby's. "You did it because Joe loves me and not you."

"You took the piano Joe gave me."

Susan stepped back, her face white. "I did not!"

Libby locked her fingers together behind her back. If Susan could lie, then so could she. "*I* didn't break that thing." She nodded at the broken figurine. "Someone else did or maybe you did it yourself and just want to make trouble for me."

"Ooooh, I could slap you!" Susan's hair bobbed as she shook her head. "I'm going to show this to Mom and Dad. They'll take care of you!"

Libby waited until Susan reached her door. "If you tell them that you even think I did it, I'll tell them you were kissing Joe."

Susan spun around, her eyes wide. "You wouldn't dare!"

"I would."

"You're not my sister! You'll never be my sister!"

Libby felt as if she'd been kicked in the stomach. She slumped to the edge of her bed. "Who wants you for a sister?"

Susan spun around and stormed out of the room. Libby sat perfectly still, her hands locked together, her chest rising and falling.

Finally she turned off her light and climbed under

the covers. She stared into the darkness and listened to her own breathing and her clock ticking on the nightstand beside her bed.

The next morning she stayed away from Susan and Susan stayed away from her. In the station wagon going to church Susan sat between Kevin and Toby while Libby sat beside Ben.

"What's wrong with you today, Elizabeth?" whispered Ben close to her ear.

"Nothing," she answered sharply. She couldn't stand Ben's kindness and patience today.

"Smile then," he said and he smiled at her. He was especially good looking in his new gray sweater and dark gray pants, Libby thought, before she turned to stare out the window.

At the church Libby rushed into the Sunday school room and sat down, putting her Bible on the seat beside her. Jill Noteboom would sit beside her today. Susan could sit with Joe, but definitely not with her!

"Good morning, Elizabeth," said Grandma Feuder as she looked up from writing on a small blackboard. "I didn't hear you come in." Grandma smiled over Libby's head. "Hello, Susan, Ben. Are you children always the first in class? Adam will be here soon. I sent him to the office to get me a better piece of chalk." Grandma tugged the skirt of her dress in place, a wide smile on her lined face. "I'm so glad that Connie asked me to teach for her today. I was sure everyone thought I was too old to be of use."

Libby sat back quietly as Susan and Ben talked to Grandma. As someone walked in Libby turned, then looked quickly straight ahead. It was Joe and he was smiling right at Susan. Libby's heart skipped a beat as

Joe sat beside Susan. Adam walked in and sat with Ben. Several others walked in just as Jill Noteboom came. She greeted Grandma, then smiled down at Libby. Jill looked ten feet tall in a flowered skirt and pink blouse.

"Hi, Libby. Thanks for saving me a seat.'"

"I'm glad you came," said Libby, making sure she smiled extra big so that Susan and Joe wouldn't think she was feeling bad.

"Mom said I could invite you to spend the day with us if your parents don't care," whispered Jill.

"I'll ask," said Libby, glad for a way to avoid seeing Susan all day long.

And when she asked, Chuck said she could and Libby thankfully walked to Jill's car with her.

"Dad said we could drive to your house so you can change your clothes," said Jill as she sat down beside Libby in the small blue car. "We're going to have a good time today, Libby. I'm going to show you my book. I've never showed it to another person, living or dead. It if doesn't bother you too much, I'd like you to answer some questions about piano and music for me."

Libby chewed the inside of her lower lip. Could she talk about piano without bursting into tears?

"Is Adam a special friend of yours?" asked Jill in a low voice.

Libby watched Adam and Ben walk across the large parking lot. "He's a friend to all of us. He and Ben play chess all the time."

"I wish he was taller. I might change my mind about boys."

Libby frowned. She didn't want to talk about boys now or any time. "Tell me about your book."

"I get it." Jill nudged Libby and giggled. "You don't want to talk about boys. I'd rather talk about my book, too, but I can't with my family coming. Wait until we get safely to my room."

Later Jill looked around Libby's room as she changed her clothes. Jill had told her to wear jeans so they could go hiking if they wanted to.

"I like your room, Libby. It makes me feel good all over. I bet it's different than most of the foster homes you've been in."

Libby's head jerked up and her hands stopped at the third button on her flowered blouse. "What do you mean?"

"I know you're a foster child, Libby. You don't have to be ashamed of it with me. I've read a great deal about foster children. I know what they have to put up with and the terrible conditions in most homes." Jill sat down on the chair near Libby's desk. "I think I know what makes you sad at times. Tell me about your other homes."

"I'd rather not." Libby didn't want to think of the homes where she'd been beaten and starved and hated. Only the Johnsons had loved her, had wanted her for a real daughter. But maybe they wouldn't if they knew how bad she'd been to Susan.

Jill touched the shiny puzzle box on Libby's desk. "I've seen pictures of puzzle boxes before, but this is the first I've seen for real. Where did you get it?"

Libby swallowed hard. "From my real dad for my twelfth birthday last Valentine's Day."

"Why don't you live with your real dad?"

Libby slowly buttoned her blouse, then tucked it into her jeans. "He's dead."

"Oh."

"But he left me his share of a ranch in the sandhills of Nebraska."

Jill's eyes sparkled. "We once lived in Nebraska in a small town called Lyons. I was in the second grade so I don't remember much about it. That was before I started writing my book." She clasped her hands together in front of her. "Oh, Libby, I can't wait to show you my book!"

"I'm ready if you are, Jill." Libby hesitated at the door, then walked out into the hall with Jill beside her. She didn't want to see Susan or talk to her.

Susan's door opened and she stood in the doorway, then jumped back and slammed the door shut.

"Is she mad at you?" asked Jill in a hushed voice that still seemed too loud to Libby. Libby nodded, but didn't say anything until they were once again in the car driving down the road.

"I'm glad Paul could stay with Kevin and Toby." Libby sat back and smiled at Jill. At last she was away from Susan! Now, she could enjoy herself. "The boys will have fun together."

"And I won't have to keep wondering if he's spying on us," said Jill.

"He doesn't spy," said Freida Noteboom, frowning over her shoulder. "I told him not to anymore."

"He doesn't always mind, Mother," said Jill, rolling her eyes. "I haven't seen a child yet who minds all the time."

Ted Noteboom looked back and winked at Libby. "Except Jill, of course. She's a perfect little angel, especially since she's been writing her book."

"What do you know about my book?" asked Jill in alarm.

"Not a thing," said Ted with a chuckle. "But I'd like to read it. I want to know how much talent you've inherited from me."

"None at all, Dad! I'm learning completely on my own."

Freida laughed. "You sound like Dad, too. He says his talent is self-taught and not real talent."

"What about you, Libby?" asked Ted. "Do you have a hidden desire to write?"

Before Libby could answer, Jill said, "Libby's going to be a concert pianist someday."

Libby groaned and sank low in the seat. How could Jill say that?

"I think that's marvelous," said Freida. "Two girls who know where they're going. How can we stand it, Ted?"

Ted stopped the car outside his garage. "I'm getting out so I don't have to stand it. Will Jill Noteboom's success spoil her famous father?" He laughed as he stepped away from the car. "Libby, don't let Jill bury you in her room all day long when it's so beautiful outside."

Jill nudged Libby. "Don't pay attention to him. He acts crazy after he's finished a new book."

After dinner Jill hurried Libby upstairs to her bedroom. She locked the door, smiled at Libby, and slowly walked to her closet. Libby watched in fascination as Jill moved aside several games and pulled out a box with a padlock on it.

"I keep my book in here." Jill pulled a chain from around her neck and Libby saw a key hooked to it. "I keep the key around my neck at all times." Slowly she inserted the key and turned it. The click was loud in the quiet room. A shiver ran down Libby's back.

"Here it is, Libby." Jill proudly held out a sheaf of papers and Libby took them. "You are the first person besides myself who has touched this book. You're the only person who'll read it until it's finished and I send it to a publisher."

"I'm afraid to touch it," said Libby, glancing down at what looked to her like ordinary typing paper with typing on it. "I don't want to ruin it, Jill."

Jill laughed and patted Libby's arm. "You won't. It's only my first draft so it won't matter if it gets smudged a little." Jill sat down on the chair beside her desk and motioned for Libby to sit on the couch. "I'll sit here quietly while you sit there and read what I've written. If you have any questions while you're reading, ask."

Libby looked at the sheaf of papers and wondered how Jill thought she could read it in such a short time. "Maybe I should take it home and read it. It'll take me a long time."

Jill frowned. "I guess you're right, Libby. Read just a couple of pages for now so you can see if you like it at all."

Libby settled back on the couch and started to read. The main character looked and sounded a lot like Jill herself. Libby was surprised that she liked what she read. It would be fun to finish reading it. She looked up with a smile and she could tell Jill was very anxious to know what she thought.

"I like it, Jill. I can't wait until I can read it all and

see what happens to Glenda Wellington."

"It isn't finished yet. After you read it, then maybe we can work together on it. Would you like that, Libby?"

She hesitated. With piano practice, she wouldn't have time for writing a book. Then she remembered that she was not going to play the piano again. A tight band seemed to squeeze her heart. "I'll help you write the book, Jill. I can help you a lot. I have plenty of free time."

No piano. No Joe. But a book. She'd work so hard on Jill's book that she wouldn't have time to think about anything else.

SIX
Everything's different

Libby stood in the empty family room and stared longingly at the piano. She clutched the locked box with Jill's book inside until her fingers hurt. Laughter drifted up from the basement where she knew Susan and Joe were playing Ping-Pong. Libby looked down at the wooden box in her hands. She would not be jealous of Susan and Joe. They could get married for all she cared!

Slowly Libby turned from the piano and walked out of the family room. How would it feel never to touch the piano again, never to hear it, or lose herself in music?

Libby wandered into the living room and looked out the window at Chuck and Vera playing soccer with the boys. Vera kicked the white and black ball and almost lost her balance.

A sad feeling of loneliness settled over Libby. Everything was different now. Her life suddenly seemed very empty. She sighed as she walked upstairs. Maybe after she got involved with Jill's book, she wouldn't feel this way.

Libby hesitated outside Susan's room. Maybe she should go in and hunt for the tiny grand piano. Shivers ran up and down her back. No, she wouldn't look for it now. Susan might come upstairs and find her. But that might be good. She could force Susan to give back the piano. Would she and Susan ever be friends again? Would they ever be sisters?

Libby frowned as she walked to her room and closed and locked her door. She set the box on her desk and laid the key on top of it. She would have to find a good hiding place for the box and the key. Jill had made her promise.

An envelope lay beside the puzzle box and Libby picked it up. She pulled out the letter and read it. It was from Grandma LaDere, her real grandma. It was very short. Grandma said she wouldn't attend Libby's recital. And oh, how glad Libby was that she hadn't come! Grandma said maybe someday she would come to hear Libby play but not now. She said Albert was just fine and that he liked the new cat food that Libby had sent him.

Libby smiled as she remembered the big blue-gray cat that didn't like anyone except herself and Grandma LaDere.

Soon Libby would answer the letter, but not while she was still feeling this bad about her failure at the recital. Should she tell Grandma LaDere that she would never play the piano again? Would Grandma even care?

"She won't. Nobody will," muttered Libby, stuffing the letter in the desk drawer where she kept letters from Mark McCall and anyone else who wrote to her. From now on when she wrote back, she'd make sure her letters were full of things about Snowball, her white filly, and school and even the weather. She wouldn't say a word about piano ever again. For sure she wouldn't tell anyone that she would never play again as long as she lived. Should she tell Mark that Susan and Joe were in love?

With a sigh Libby unlocked the box and lifted out the typed pages. She would read as much as she could before she had to do chores. Maybe she'd learn to enjoy writing and not miss being a famous concert pianist. Maybe!

After several pages Libby discovered that Glenda Wellington was too tall and ugly to attract men but she was a famous murder mystery author who helped the police solve murders. The murder was described in bloody, gory detail. Jill sure liked to paint a clear picture with her words. Libby wrinkled her nose and wondered if she could help write such a book. When Jill introduced the man who played the piano, Libby dropped the pages onto her bed and paced across the carpeted floor.

She stopped at her window and stared out at the sheep pen. She remembered the time Brenda Wilkens had unhooked the gate and let the sheep out, then blamed it on her. But now Brenda was her friend. It seemed strange not to have her hanging around Ben all the time. She had a boyfriend now who was three years older than she was and she acted as if she'd forgotten that Ben was alive. All she could talk about was, Tom, Tom, Tom, Tom.

Was Susan turning into another Brenda? Would Susan talk about boys, particularly Joe Wilkens, from now on?

Libby thought about her real cousin Tammy LaDere. *She* could only think of boys too.

"*That* will never happen to me!" she whispered fiercely. Abruptly she walked to her bed and picked up the scattered pages. She sat on the floor with her knees pulled up to her chin and started reading again. To be Jill's friend, she'd have to read the book, then help Jill with it. Right now Jill was the only friend she had.

Finally Libby stopped reading and put the book back in the box and locked it securely. She looked around the room with a thoughtful frown. Where could she hide the box and the key so that no one would find it even if they looked for it? Jill could not survive, she'd said, if anything happened to her precious book. She said that she'd pick it up after school tomorrow.

Finally Libby pushed the box into the corner of her closet shelf, then opened the puzzle box and put the key inside. She smiled. Even Jill would think it was well taken care of.

Someone knocked on the door and Libby jumped. She hurried to open it, then hesitated. Was it Susan? "Who is it?"

"Me, Elizabeth."

Chuck! Libby quickly unlocked the door and pulled it open. Her face felt hot and she wondered if she looked guilty. "Hi, Dad."

"What're you doing locked away in your room, Elizabeth? Are you sick? Did you get overtired at Jill's house?"

"I'm all right, Dad. I just wanted to be alone."

Chuck hooked his thumb in his jeans pocket and grinned. "What's the dark secret?"

"Nothing," she said quickly, too quickly.

"Hey, don't get flustered. I'm joking. Come on down and help with chores. The horses wouldn't know what to do without you." He chuckled and Libby felt a laugh rise up inside her.

Chuck laid his arm across her shoulders as they walked down the hall. "Ms. Kremeen stopped in at the store yesterday to see me." Libby stumbled and Chuck caught her. "Don't let that scare you, honey. She just wanted to let me know that the adoption should go through soon. She said the judge will want to talk to you first before he signs the final decree."

Libby's mouth felt very dry and her throat closed around the words that she tried to speak.

"Don't get scared, Elizabeth." Chuck stopped at the top of the stairs and turned Libby to him. "We prayed you into this family. Nothing will keep you from becoming a Johnson. Nothing!"

She swallowed hard and tears stung her eyes. "Dad, you don't know how bad I've been."

"Good or bad, honey, you belong to us. We love you."

"What if . . . if I can't be a famous pianist?" She saw the laugh lines at the corners of his eyes deepen and spread to his hairline. His hair was almost as red as Ben's and Toby's.

"Elizabeth, you belong to us no matter what you do or how you act. You belong to this family."

She knew he wouldn't feel that way if Susan told on her. But Susan couldn't tell.

"I know something's bothering you, Elizabeth. When you're ready to talk about it, I'm ready to listen."

She nodded, then started down the stairs.

"I hope you aren't worried about your real mother."

Libby looked over her shoulder, waiting, her hand tight around the smooth banister.

"She's gone again. Ms. Kremeen said she went to Reno with a man. Maybe this time she'll stay away. But even if she doesn't, she signed the papers giving you up for adoption." Chuck squeezed her shoulder. "And we're going to adopt you. That's the truth, young lady with the hazel eyes."

Libby turned with a giggle. The giggle died in her throat as Susan started up the stairs. Libby wondered if Chuck noticed the angry look that Susan had shot her.

"Time to do chores, Susan," he said, tugging the ponytail over her left ear.

"Don't do that, Dad!" She shook her head and frowned.

"Is something wrong, honey?"

"Ask your precious Elizabeth!" She dashed away, then a door slammed and Libby knew Susan was in her room, probably kicking something and wishing it was Libby.

The grandfather clock bonged six just as Libby reached the bottom of the steps. Chuck caught her hand and tugged her to a stop.

"Are you and Susan fighting about something?"

"Ask Susan," she said stiffly.

"I'm asking you." He frowned. "What's going on?"

With her free hand Libby rubbed her jeans. Frantically she searched her mind for something to say. "I . . . I guess Susan is mad because she thinks I like Joe and she does too."

Chuck looked up at the ceiling. "Boys already! I must be getting old. You and Susan seem too young to like

boys." Chuck shook his head and walked away.

Libby looked upstairs, then followed Chuck. She stopped in the open doorway of the family room and looked unhappily at the silent piano. Soon Joanne Tripper would be taking piano lessons from Rachael Avery and the forgotten Elizabeth Gail Dobbs would be left to find a dreary life for herself. Oh, how could she stand to see Joanne Tripper come to school each day and brag about how good she was and how much Rachael loved her and helped her?

Libby bit her lower lip to keep from crying out. She would not tell Joanne or Rachael that she was quitting piano until she absolutely had to. And that wouldn't be until the first Saturday in December.

Rachael had planned to be on vacation just after the recital.

Libby lifted her head and squared her shoulders. By then she would have new interests. By then it wouldn't hurt so much to quit lessons with Rachael and watch Joanne step into her empty place.

"Who cares anyway?" whispered Libby, blinking hard to keep the tears back. "I hate piano!"

SEVEN
Joanne Tripper

Libby turned her back to the cold wind as she waited at the end of the driveway for the school bus. The sky was gray and theatened rain or maybe even snow. Libby knew Ben was anxious for snow so that after Thanksgiving he could use the sleigh to take families back to the stand of blue spruce to choose their Christmas trees.

"Libby."

Libby turned to find Susan standing hesitantly beside her, a strained look on her face. "What?"

"I don't want to be mad anymore."

Libby hesitated. She really didn't want to be mad either, but was Susan saying she was sorry for taking the tiny piano? "I don't either."

"Let's forget what's happened."

Libby gnawed her lower lip for a minute, then said, "All right." She cleared her throat. "I wish you would forget about boys."

"Joe, you mean," snapped Susan.

"I don't! I don't," she said again in a low tight voice.

How could Susan think that? Maybe she was right. Libby pushed the thought aside so she wouldn't think about it at all.

"I can't be like you, Libby. I can't bury myself in the piano all day long and forget about everything else."

Libby turned away, her heart racing. She wouldn't be doing that again. How could she bear it?

"Here comes the bus!" yelled Toby.

Libby thankfully stepped behind Ben and away from Susan. Rex barked from his doghouse and a horse whinnied.

Libby climbed on the half-filled bus and walked toward the back. She turned her head away when Joe said hello. Susan would sit with him and maybe hold hands. Brenda sat with another high school girl. Libby found an empty seat and sat down just as the bus lurched. She'd save a place for Jill as she'd promised yesterday.

Just as the bus stopped for Jill and Paul, Susan hurried back to Libby and dropped a folded paper in her lap. Libby looked up in surprise, then opened the paper, her eyes on Susan as she sat back down beside Joe.

Libby looked down at the scrawled writing. "I did not take your stupid piano. Stop blaming me." It was signed "Susan."

"What's up, Libby?" asked Jill, dropping down beside Libby. Jill was dressed in navy blue slacks. She pushed the hood of her blue and white jacket off her head.

"You're cold, Jill." Libby moved away so that she couldn't feel Jill.

"You're changing the subject, Libby. When I sat down

you had your mouth hanging wide open and you quickly wadded up that paper you were reading. Is our friendship starting out with secrets between us?"

"I read your book." Libby had to keep Jill's mind off Susan's note for a while. The note felt sharp against Libby's palm. Should she believe Susan? If so, who took the piano from her drawer?

"Hey, Libby. I'm talking to you." Jill nudged Libby sharply. "I can see you have a lot on your mind. Is it too private to talk about?"

Libby nodded. She ducked out of the way of a paper wad.

"I guess you aren't ready to share yourself with me." Jill sighed and shook her head. "I wanted us to be best friends, Libby. I've never had a best friend before. Nobody wants to be best friends with an elephant."

Libby frowned. "Elephant?" Everyone was so noisy it was hard to hear.

"Me! I'd give anything to be short and thin like you."

"Oh, sure. You mean short and pretty like Susan." Beside Susan, Libby always felt tall and skinny and ugly. Beside Jill, Libby felt *short* and skinny and ugly.

"You're right. We could go on this way all day long but where would it get us? I'm tall and big and I might as well get used to it." She slipped down low in the seat and grinned at Libby. "You said you read my book. What did you think?"

Libby frowned at little Trina Bowers until she finally turned back around in her seat and sat down. "You described things really well, Jill."

"I did, didn't I?" Jill smiled. "I know that book will sell. I just might make it by the time I'm fourteen! Famous Jill Noteboom, author." She tapped Libby's leg.

"You could have your name on it too if you help me enough."

Libby shrugged. "I don't know. I don't think I have enough words inside me."

"Sure you do. We just have to get them out, then down on paper." Jill's eyes narrowed. "What's on the paper in your hand?"

Quickly Libby stuffed it in her jacket pocket. "Maybe I'll tell you later."

"Is it a love note?"

Libby flushed. "Of course not!"

"I wonder if Susan and Joe write love notes back and forth."

"They love each other," whispered Libby painfully. She stared at her tan cords, her heart hammering.

Jill leaned close to Libby's ear. "Did you love Joe?"

Just then the bus stopped at a railroad crossing and everyone was absolutely still. Libby wondered if they could hear her heart beating. Did anyone notice her flushed face? How could she answer Jill?

The bus crossed the tracks and everyone started talking at once. Jill nudged Libby. "Were you in love with him?"

Libby licked her dry lips. "Maybe."

"And now Susan is."

"Yes."

"So, who needs boys? We'll become successful first and then men will fall all over us. Dad says successful women attract men."

Libby stared out the window and watched as the bus turned into the school drive. She was beginning to think Jill thought more about boys than her precious book.

"Save me a seat if you get on the bus tonight before I do," said Jill as she stood. "I'll do the same."

Libby nodded, then slowly stepped in line to get off the bus. An elbow jabbed in her back and she turned with a frown. It was Adam and he laughed. "Hi, Adam."

"I thought you'd forgotten my name. You didn't speak to me when I got on the bus."

"Sorry." She wrinkled her nose.

"You'd better be. I'm coming over again tonight."

She smiled. "Want to play Ping-Pong? I'm getting very good."

"Ben and I are playing chess again. Why don't you learn, Elizabeth? You'd like it."

She stepped into the cold air and walked away from Adam without another word. How many years would Adam and Ben play chess? Adam had been her friend first. It just wasn't fair.

The noise in the hallway rang through her head as she walked to her locker and hung up her jacket. She pulled out the books she needed and banged the door shut. She turned around and stopped abruptly. Joanne Tripper blocked her way.

"I was at the recital Friday night," said Joanne, bursting into laughter. "I heard you, Libby." Joanne's blonde hair hung long and pretty around her slender shoulders and down her back. The blue blouse matched her eyes and the blue plaid skirt fit snugly around her hips, then flared out to show off her shapely legs. Libby knew Joanne loved to show off her good figure.

"Let me pass," said Libby stiffly.

"Not until I'm done talking to you." Joanne tossed

her head. "I'm surprised that Rachael Avery even admitted that you were her student. You should know by now that I should be the one to take lessons from her. *I* would have performed beautifully. Momma said so. And Momma made sure she talked to Rachael Avery after the recital. Momma told her all about my ability at piano."

"I'll bet she did."

"And Rachael was very interested. She had already promised to take me as a student when she could, but she was very glad to meet me in person. *I* think you know it's time to stop taking lessons with her and let me. You could take from just anybody and it wouldn't matter. But I can't! I need the best!"

"Joanne, would you like a punch in the nose?" asked Libby in a low, tight voice. "I'm ready to hit you. Move right now."

Joanne stepped back nervously, clutching her books to her chest. "My, my. You sound like I'd expect an aid kid to sound. I wonder how the Johnsons put up with you."

Libby gripped her books so tightly she thought her fingers would break. She wanted to sock Joanne right in the nose and make blood spurt all over her beautiful clothes. But she couldn't do that. The old Libby would have, but she was a new creature in Christ. She was learning to live in love, not hatred and anger. "Get away and leave me alone, Joanne. I mean it."

"Having trouble, Libby?"

Jill stood beside Joanne and seemed to tower over her.

"Joanne won't let me pass and I'll be late for class."

Jill frowned down at Joanne. Libby saw Joanne's face

turn white. "Get out of the way, Joanne whoever you are."

"This is none of your business, giant," said Joanne icily.

Libby gasped and wondered what Jill would do. The hall suddenly seemed very quiet.

Jill looked down at Joanne. "How does it feel to be a short snob?"

Joanne glared at her, then at Libby, and turned and walked away, her head high.

The warning bell rang and Libby laughed nervously. "Thanks, Jill."

"That's all right. We tall people have to stick together." She grinned, then hurried away down the hall.

Libby rushed to class and sat down just as the final bell rang. For a while she wouldn't have to think about Joanne Tripper or Susan or the note stuffed in her jacket pocket.

EIGHT
Thanksgiving Day

Reluctantly Libby opened her eyes. For three days Joanne Tripper had harassed her about the recital. Today she couldn't take it. And then she remembered that it was Thanksgiving Day and she jumped out of bed, a laugh bubbling up inside. Today she wouldn't have to put up with Joanne Tripper. Today Susan would be nice to her. Last night they'd decided to try harder to be friends again.

"But I still say you took my tiny piano," Libby had said sharply.

Susan had shrugged. "Believe what you want. I didn't and I don't have it, but I won't fight again about it. And I do love Joe and he loves me and that's the way it is!"

Libby had decided to ignore Susan and Joe altogether. Maybe someday Susan would decide that Joe wasn't that much fun to be around and Libby would have a sister again.

In the bathroom Libby turned on the shower, waited until it was steamy warm and stepped inside. The water beat against her, making a song rise inside. She wanted to sing at the top of her lungs but it would be very embarrassing if anyone heard, so she sang practically under her breath. She poured thick yellow shampoo into her hand and rubbed it into her hair. She remembered one foster home where she'd only been allowed a bath once a week and a shampoo every two weeks. Vera insisted that she take a shower and shampoo every day.

"We don't want you smelling like the horses," Vera had said, laughing.

It had made Libby feel cared for when Vera had showed her how to trim her fingernails and toenails, then taught her to keep them clean.

Later in her room Libby pulled on clean jeans and a sweatshirt. Today the family was going on a wagon ride while the turkey roasted in the oven. Chuck had said he would hitch Jack and Dan, the big gray draft horses, to the wagon and ride out to check Ben's Christmas trees. Chuck had said they could mark the tree that they wanted for their own Christmas tree.

As she hurried downstairs Libby remembered last Thanksgiving when Kevin had introduced her to Grandma and Grandpa Johnson as a big surprise. Susan had had to stay in bed all that day. But today everyone was well. The grandparents couldn't come for Thanksgiving, but promised to come at Christmas. Uncle Luke, Aunt Gwen, and Scottie were coming too.

Cold wind blew against Libby as she walked across the yard toward the horse barn. Ben was probably already in the cow barn doing the milking. The barn door was open and Libby walked in to find Chuck standing by Dan's stall. He turned with a smile when he saw Libby.

"Good morning, Elizabeth. This is going to be a beautiful day. Dan tells me he will be glad to pull the wagon to the back of our property today. He said he'd let Jack come along to help."

Libby laughed as she reached into the stall and patted the big gray's neck. Once she'd been very frightened of the big team, but she soon learned that they were more gentle than any of the other horses.

Apache Girl nickered and Snowball answered. Libby reached in her jacket pocket and brought out two apples. "Thanksgiving treat," she said as she grinned sheepishly up at Chuck. "They love apples."

"I know. I brought a few out too." He walked down the concrete aisle to Snowball's stall.

"Here, Snowball." Libby handed her filly an apple. Snowball's soft lips touched Libby's palm and then the apple was gone.

Chuck slipped his arm around Libby's shoulders as they walked to Apache Girl's stall and handed her an apple. "I told Susan she could invite Joe on the wagon ride today, Elizabeth. I hope it won't bother you."

She swallowed hard and kept her eyes on the barn cat that slept on a bale of hay in an empty stall. "I don't mind." But did she? And why did it hurt so much?

"Growing up isn't simple, Elizabeth. Just remember that while you're growing up, Jesus is always with you to help you. At times you won't understand yourself, the way you feel or even the way you act. Ask the Lord to help you then, too. He knows all about you. He'll help you understand yourself."

She brushed a piece of straw off her sleeve. "Dad. . . ."

"Yes."

She looked up, then quickly down at her boots. "Sometimes I hate Susan."

"It's not always easy to love others, even–or maybe especially–sisters," said Chuck, as he smiled into her eyes. "But Jesus tells us to love others, and he gives us the strength to help us carry out his commands. I don't know what Susan's done to you, but Jesus can help you love her and forgive her."

Libby thought about what Chuck had said in the barn while she finished her chores, then ate breakfast. She knew Chuck was right, but she wasn't quite ready to have the Lord help her. Susan deserved to be hated just a little.

Chuck set down his cup of coffee. "Ben, if you want to invite someone on our ride, you may. Elizabeth, same with you. And you two little boys with your mouths full of pancakes can ask Paul Noteboom if you want."

Kevin swallowed and his eyes twinkled behind his glasses. "Ben can ask Jill, and Libby, Adam."

"It'll be the other way around," said Ben with a frown. "Who wants to invite a girl who's ten feet tall?"

"She isn't that tall!" cried Libby.

"Almost," said Susan, making a face. "And she's really weird."

"You're weird youself," snapped Libby.

"Children!" warned Vera. "Today we're going to have a beautiful day. We won't have any fighting or arguing. Is that clear?"

Libby nodded and the others mumbled in agreement. Libby always felt surprised at how well the Johnson kids minded. Once she'd asked Vera why they were so good.

"Chuck and I always pray for each of you children," she had said with a smile. "We agree together that you'll always be the best you can be. And God gives us wisdom to help you."

Libby looked up at Vera as she stood up and reached for the plates. A warm feeling spread inside Libby. If she ever became a mother, she wanted to be just like Vera.

An hour later Libby sat in the wagon with Jill beside her. Adam sat with Ben and they were discussing how easily Ben had checkmated Adam. Paul jumped around with Kevin and Toby until Vera told them to sit down. Toby bumped into Susan and knocked her against Joe. Her face flushed a bright red, but Libby knew she'd enjoyed being knocked against him.

"I wrote more in my book," whispered Jill as Chuck slapped the reins on the team's backs.

"That's good," said Libby, forcing her eyes away from Susan and Joe.

"Glenda is just ready to solve the murder. Can you guess who it is, Libby? Did I plant my clues right?"

Libby tried to sound excited as they discussed the book.

"There's a deer!" shouted Paul, almost toppling from the wagon as he jumped up and down. Kevin tugged him by the jacket until he plopped back down.

"Look at that white tail!" Jill turned and watched until the deer leaped out of sight among the trees. She turned back to Libby and her dark eyes were sparkling excitedly. "Oh, Libby, I'm so glad you invited me today. That is the first time I've seen a deer that close. And its tail is so big! Someday I want to come here on a hike with you and we'll find a hiding place where we can stay until a deer walks right up to us. I would like to know all about deer. Maybe I'll put them in my book."

Libby giggled and Jill asked her what was so funny. "You always think about that book, don't you?"

Jill shrugged. "I guess so."

"That's how I am with . . . with. . . ." Her voice died away and tears stung her eyes.

"With what, Libby? With Joe?" whispered Jill.

Libby looked quickly at Joe, then down at her hands. "No! I'm not like Susan. I have more important things to think about."

Jill moved closer to Libby. "You mean this has something to do with piano?"

Libby flushed. Should she tell Jill how she felt?

Just then Chuck yelled for Jack and Dan to stop. Everyone jumped from the wagon with Libby and Jill out last.

"Your trees have grown, Ben," said Chuck, pulling off his gloves. "I think you'll have to sell all of those in that area."

"I'lll help you with your business if you want," said Adam excitedly.

Ben looked quickly at Libby and she just knew he was going to say that he already had the best help he could get, but he smiled at Adam and said that was the best idea he'd ever heard.

Libby walked quickly away and she knew Jill was right beside her. How could Ben do this to her? Didn't he like her anymore? Hadn't she done a very good job last year after all?

"What's wrong?" asked Jill in a low concerned voice.

Libby shrugged.

"Libby, talk to me. Are we best friends or not?"

Libby hesitated. Was Jill her best friend? Libby opened her mouth, then closed it. She just couldn't tell Jill how she felt. Jill might tell. And that would be awful!

"Don't you trust me yet, Libby? I wish you would. What can I do?"

Libby looked up at Jill. "We are friends, Jill, but I can't talk about myself. Maybe someday. I don't know how you can tell your feelings the way you do."

Jill hunched her shoulders. "Mom says telling your feelings is a way of sharing yourself with others. I don't tell my feelings to just anyone, Libby. But I trust you. You don't think I'm weird like most kids do. You don't make fun of my size."

Something inside Libby melted and she smiled. She could trust Jill. Jill wouldn't make fun of her or blab her secrets. "Let's walk over there so nobody can hear what I say," Libby said softly.

"I won't even put what you're going to tell me in my books, Libby."

"Thanks."

"I won't even use it as a story idea."

Libby laughed and Jill did too.

A red cardinal landed on a branch, then flew away. The three little boys ran and shouted and played among the trees.

Libby took a deep breath, then let it out. "Jill, I'm a failure." The words hurt her throat. Slowly, bit by bit, with a little urging from Jill, Libby told about the recital and her decision never to play the piano again.

"And I thought all this was because of Susan and Joe." Jill shook her head. "I'm really sorry about the recital."

"Me too."

"I guess you'd rather break your fingers than give up piano."

Libby nodded. She knew if she tried to talk she'd burst into tears.

"Maybe if you work on my book you might be able to forget easier."

"Maybe." But Libby knew nothing would make her forget.

"Time to go!" shouted Chuck, waving at them. "All aboard. The turkey is waiting!"

Jill touched Libby's arm. "You have a happy Thanksgiving anyway, okay?"

Libby nodded, then managed a smile. "I'm glad we're best friends."

NINE
Piano

Libby paced restlessly from the family room where Ben was gluing a model and the little boys were playing checkers noisily, to the quiet living room, then to the kitchen. She would've gone in the study but Chuck and Vera were inside talking.

Smells of the big Thanksgiving dinner still floated through the air. The house was warm but, for some reason, not cozy today. She walked down to the basement and ran her hand across the Ping-Pong table, then sat down in the rocker in front of the large stone fireplace. But she couldn't stay still for long. She pushed her brown hair back in jerky movements. The neck of her pink sweater suddenly seemed too tight and she tugged at it.

Why, oh why had she told Jill about the piano? If Jill didn't keep her secret, everyone would know soon. Libby groaned and shook her head. She'd have to tell Chuck and Vera soon anyway. She'd have to tell Rachael Avery just as soon as she got back from vacation. Rachael would probably be relieved. It would keep her from having to let her go.

Libby walked to the stairs and slowly climbed them. She stopped at the top and stared down at her long, slender fingers. Piano fingers, Chuck had called them.

Tears stung Libby's eyes and she quickly blinked them away. She would not cry! What kind of baby was she?

Suddenly Toby shouted that he won and Kevin cried that he'd cheated, then Ben told them to stop it or they'd get it from Dad. As Libby stopped in the doorway, they looked up guiltily, then laughed. She knew they'd expected Chuck or Vera. Kevin and Toby pushed past her and ran to the back porch.

"Why aren't you practicing?" asked Ben.

"I just don't feel like it."

The back door slammed and Libby knew the boys had gone out to play, probably soccer.

"Where's Susan?" Ben looked around in case she was in the family room and he'd missed her.

"Reading in her room." Libby stood at the window and looked out. Joe had to go away with his family or he'd be here and Susan would be with him. Libby walked over to stand in front of the crackling fire, then to the piano, and quickly away from it to sit down on Vera's favorite chair.

"What's wrong, Elizabeth?" Ben capped the glue and laid it in the box.

"What makes you think something's wrong?"

"You act like you don't have anything to do."

"I'm bored."

"You?" Ben's red eyebrows almost met his hair as he raised them in surprise.

"What's so surprising about that?" Libby pushed her hands against her bony knees. "I don't like putting models together. Susan doesn't want me around her. And I sure don't want to play soccer with the boys."

"Play the piano. That's what you're always doing."

Hadn't he noticed that she hadn't touched the piano since last Friday night? "I don't feel like it."

"What's wrong? You never felt like that before."

"I can change, can't I?" She jumped up and walked to the window again. "You don't do the same thing every day and every day!"

"I'm not planning on being a concert pianist."

She spun around to see what he meant by that but he was busily cleaning up his mess. She bit her tongue to keep from saying that she wasn't planning on being a concert pianist either.

Ben looked up and smiled. "Want to ride back to the Christmas trees with me in the morning?"

A cold band seemed to tighten around her heart. "I didn't think you'd want me to since Adam's going to help you this season."

Ben walked to her and shook his head. "I didn't mean to upset you, Elizabeth. I thought you'd be too busy with piano to work with me."

She opened her mouth, then closed it. She could not tell him! He sounded proud of her for wanting to be a concert pianist. "You're right," she said in a low voice.

"I've got to put this stuff away. Maybe we could play a game later."

"Maybe." She stood by the game table until Ben walked out of the room, then slowly she walked to the piano. She touched it, then gently pressed a key.

"I've been meaning to talk to you about that."

Libby swung around, startled, wondering what Vera meant.

Vera walked slowly to the piano, then smiled at Libby. "Honey, you can't stop practicing just because you don't take lessons right now. You must keep at it so that when Rachael comes back, you'll be ready."

Libby couldn't talk around the lump in her throat. She pushed her hands deep into her jeans pockets and barely nodded.

"I miss hearing you." Vera slipped her arm around Libby's waist. "I wanted so badly to have Susan take lessons, but she was determined not to. Then you came to live with us and you wanted to. It made me very happy. I know how much enjoyment you can get and give out of playing the piano." Vera turned Libby to her. "I like to see you sitting at the piano. I like to listen to you play even though you're still learning."

Libby wanted to run from the room and lock herself into her bedroom, but she stood very still, her eyes on the piano and her hands in her pockets.

"Oh! Oh, Libby!" Vera shook her head. "I have been meaning to tell you that I found your tiny piano that Joe gave you."

Libby's eyes widened. "Where?"

"In your drawer when I was putting away your clothes. I saw that a leg was broken on it so I brought it down to glue it."

Susan hadn't taken it! Libby's head felt as if it would explode from the inside out. She'd broken Susan's figurine to get even and Susan hadn't even done anything to her!

"What's the matter, Libby?"

She cleared her throat. "Where is it now?"

"In the kitchen on the windowsill," Vera said with a puzzled frown.

Libby dashed away, then frantically searched the windowsills in the kitchen. She turned at a step behind her. "Where, Mom?"

"Right there. Oh! It's gone! But I put it there so the glue would dry. And then I was going to take it back to your room." Vera looked on the counters and around her plants while Libby waited, her heart barely beating. Vera turned to her again. "Maybe one of the kids took it to your room."

Libby shook her head. "It's not there."

"Then where is it?"

Libby cleared her throat. "I'll ask the others." Meaning Susan. And this time Susan wouldn't get out of it so easily. No one but Susan would even want the tiny piano.

"Don't worry, Elizabeth, we'll find it." Vera patted her arm and smiled.

"I know we will," said Libby grimly, walking out of the kitchen.

Her legs felt weak as she knocked on Susan's door.

"Who is it?"

Libby knocked again.

"Toby, if you're playing another trick on me, I'll get you good!" Susan flung open the door, then blinked in surprise. "Why didn't you answer me?"

"Where's the piano?"

Susan closed her eyes and turned away. "Not that again!"

"Susan! Where is the piano? Mom took it from my room and left it in the kitchen. It's gone from there. Where is it? Did you smash it? Did you take it and pretend Joe gave it to you instead of me?"

Susan spun around, her blue eyes bright with anger.

"No! I don't need to! Joe gave me something, something a lot better than that stupid little piano."

"Where is the piano?" Libby clenched her fists and stepped close to Susan. "I want it now!"

"Then get out of here and go find it!" Susan pushed against her and Libby stumbled back, her eyes wide in surprise. Susan had pushed her! Susan didn't do things like that! None of the Johnsons did.

"What's going on here, girls?"

Libby looked up to find Chuck frowning down at her. Libby's shoulders tensed and she ducked her head.

"Libby thinks I took her piano and I didn't," Susan said angrily. "I told her to look for it somewhere else."

"What piano?" asked Chuck, looping his thumbs in the pockets of his faded jeans.

"The one Joe gave me," said Libby in a strained voice.

Chuck looked from Susan to Libby. "Girls, the Lord knows where that piano is. We'll agree right now in the name of Jesus that we'll find it and find it soon. We can't have strife in our home. Our home is full of God's love."

Libby peeked at Susan to find her in tears. Let her cry! Libby knew in her heart that Susan had taken the piano and she was determined to find a way to make her tell. Libby nodded. Susan would tell. She sure would!

TEN
The missing book

Libby held Teddy close as Jill paced the bedroom floor, thoughtfully chewing the eraser of her yellow pencil. Suddenly Jill stopped, her eyes wide. The afternoon sun made her brown hair look almost blonde.

"I have it, Libby! Finally I have it!"

"What?" Libby leaned forward expectantly.

"Glenda meets this great guy and falls in love but he turns out to be the murderer."

"Does she have to fall in love?"

Jill grinned. "You describe the man and I'll write it down." She poised her pencil over the sheaf of papers. "Make it good, Libby."

Suddenly the bedroom door opened and Susan walked in. Libby jumped up and Jill quickly hid the papers behind her back.

"What do you want, Susan?" asked Libby impatiently.

"Mom said Joe called this morning, and that you answered the phone."

Libby shrugged and tried to appear very calm even

though her heart was racing. "So? Did you want me to drag you out of the shower?" She saw the stricken look on Susan's face and felt sorry for a minute.

"But you knew he was at his Grandma's and was calling long distance! You knew he wouldn't have a chance to call me again!" Susan's voice rose and Libby knew she was ready to burst into tears. "And I can't call him back!"

"He'll be back Sunday, Susan. He said so."

"But I can't wait that long! Oh, Libby! How could you do this to me? How could you?" Susan burst into tears and ran from the room, slamming the door with a loud bang.

Libby turned to Jill. "Sorry about that."

"That's all right. I got it all down."

Libby frowned and Jill told her it was important to write down emotions when she saw them or felt them. "And Susan sure was feeling! She likes Joe a lot, doesn't she?"

Libby nodded, trying to hear Susan's sobbing from the room next door. She could only hear the scratching of Jill's pencil and her own heart. Oh, she should've told Susan about the call! She should've gotten her from the shower. But how was she to know a stupid phone call from Joe was that important to Susan?

"What are you thinking about now, Libby?" asked Jill impatiently. "I'm here for us to work on my book. Shall we work or not?"

Libby knew she couldn't concentrate with Susan right down the hall. "Let's go to the horse barn, Jill. We'll have plenty of privacy and I'll be able to think better."

"A barn should be a very interesting place to work

from." Jill nodded thoughtfully. "I'll just take the manuscript and a couple of pencils. I'll leave the box here and get it before I go home."

Libby tried not to hesitate as they walked past Susan's door, but she couldn't help herself. Jill looked back impatiently and she hurried on. Would it always be this way with Susan? A sadness filled Libby, starting deep inside. What had happened to bouncy, laughing Susan Johnson? Libby forced the thought away and slipped on her jacket and boots. Right now she was going to work on Jill's book.

Snowball nickered from the pen outside the barn, then stuck her nose over the fence. Libby patted her and introduced her to Jill. Apache Girl pushed up beside Snowball and Libby rubbed her neck.

"My brother wants a horse of his own," said Jill as she waited beside the barn door. "I would but I don't think a horse could take my weight on his back."

"Oh, Jill." Libby didn't notice Jill's size now that they were friends.

"Dad says I shouldn't put myself down. I said I'd try not to but I forget." She hunched her shoulders and Libby caught a yearning look on her face.

They walked into the barn and Libby closed the door against the cold air. A barn cat mewed and ran to rub himself against Libby's leg.

"We'll sit behind those bales of hay." Libby pointed at the hay in an empty stall. She remembered the day in September when she'd discovered April and May Brakie hiding there. Jill would like the twins. Right after Thanksgiving vacation she'd introduce Jill to them.

Jill settled herself down and pulled out her pencil.

"Describe the man who falls in love with Glenda Wellington, Libby."

Libby screwed up her face and drummed her fingers on her legs. "Should he be tall or short?"

"Tall. Very tall."

"Dark hair or blond?"

"Light brown like Adam's and curly like his."

Libby glanced sharply at Jill and caught a soft look on her face, a look that she'd seen often on Susan's face when she was talking about Joe. Oh, how could this be? What was wrong with Jill?

"What's wrong with you, Libby?"

"Not a thing! But I'm not sure about you."

Jill frowned and tried to act innocent and Libby wanted to scream at her. "I don't know what you're talking about," Jill said.

"And I thought we were best friends and shared all our feelings and thoughts."

Jill flushed and Libby turned away with a scowl. "Let's talk about this man and not me." Jill tapped the page. "More descriptions, Libby."

Libby opened her mouth but before she could speak, the barn door burst open and Paul Noteboom rushed in. "Jill! Hurry, Jill. Dad called and we have to go home right this minute. He has to go to town and he wants us to go with him. Hurry."

Jill stood hesitantly beside the bale of hay, her manuscript clutched in her hands. "I have to get my box for this."

"Come on, Jill. Dad said now!"

"Give it to me and I'll lock it away," said Libby, holding out her hand. "I'll take good care of it and you can get it tomorrow or Sunday."

Jill pushed the papers into Libby's hand. "But don't let anyone read this. Don't let it out of your sight unless it's locked away in the box."

"I won't."

"Hurry up, Jill. Dad said it's important." Paul jumped from one foot to another. "Hurry."

"All right, Paul. Don't get so impatient." Jill rushed away with Paul, calling good-bye over her shoulder.

Libby sat on one bale of hay and leaned back on another. A cat crawled onto her lap and she stroked it gently. The manuscript lay beside her. She looked at her long, slender fingers against the cat's gold hair. How long would it take her fingers to grow stiff and unable to play the piano?

She jumped up and walked to the back door of the barn. She opened it and Snowball walked in. She slipped her arms around the white filly's neck and hugged her. Snowball smelled dusty and cold. Her winter coat was long and furry already.

"I really don't want to stop playing piano, Snowball, but I must. I can't play and I'll never be able to play. I wish you could understand me and talk to me." Snowball bobbed her head up and down and Libby laughed softly. "I guess maybe you understand me a little, don't you?"

Libby opened the stall door and Snowball walked inside. Libby found the brush and brushed the white mane and tail. Just as she finished Toby ran into the barn.

He stopped at the stall with a frown, his hands on his hips. "Mom has been calling you, Libby. Why didn't you answer?"

"I didn't hear, that's why!" Libby put the brush on

the shelf and followed Toby outdoors. Dark clouds blocked out the sun and Libby shivered, pulling her hood over her head. Suddenly she stopped. "Tell Mom I'll be right there."

"She said hurry fast, Libby."

"I will," she called over her shoulder as she rushed back into the barn. She picked up Jill's book and rushed out, skirting a wide mud puddle. Maybe it would snow tonight.

"Libby! Come here quickly!"

Libby turned at the sound of Vera's frantic voice. Vera stood in the open door of the cow barn, motioning to Libby. She dropped the papers on the picnic table near the back door and rushed to Vera.

"Libby, a calf got hurt and Ben's not here to help. Please, get the salve and help me doctor it."

Later Vera held the calf while Libby smeared the thick, smelly salve on the deep cut. She remembered doctoring Snowball when she was small. The family said that Libby had a way with animals and she'd always been given the job of doctoring them.

"Thanks, Libby." Vera rubbed her fingers on a tissue from her pocket. "I thought I could take care of the calf myself but I am not quite strong enough."

"I don't think the cut is deep enough to need stitches. I'll doctor him again when I feed him later."

"You're a wonderful girl, Libby. I'm thankful that you like animals as much as you do." Vera leaned against the stall door and watched the calf. "When I was a little girl I wanted to have a farm and lots of animals. While I was in college I almost gave up my dream to study music. Then Chuck came along and I fell in love with him and married him and we bought this place. I never regretted it. Some of my friends ask me how I stand living in the country and not in the city where I could get a job." Vera smiled at Libby. "I am happy here, Libby. I can tell that you are too. I know that you won't always live on the farm. A concert pianist can't. But the farm will always pull you back, even if only to visit."

Libby looked down at the toes of her boots as she fought against the sick feeling in her stomach. Soon Vera would have to know the truth. It would be very hard to tell her.

Vera lifted her head. "Listen. The wind came up. I heard that it is supposed to snow and blow. I hope we don't get snowed in."

Libby clapped her hand to her mouth. "Oh, no! I forgot Jill's book!" She ran from the barn, the wind whipping against her. She reached the picnic table, frantically looking around. The pile of papers was gone! She looked around the area nearby. Where had the wind blown the papers? Her heart raced painfully.

"Did you find the book?" asked Vera.

Libby turned to her. "No! It's gone!"

"Maybe one of the kids took it in."

"Maybe! Oh, I hope so!" She dashed to the back porch and yelled as loud as she could. Kevin and Toby almost fell over each other running to her. Quickly, breathlessly she asked if they'd seen the papers on the picnic table. Her stomach cramped painfully as they answered no. "Where is Susan? Maybe she took them."

Kevin and Toby looked at each other and shrugged, then Kevin said, "I think she's in her room. I didn't see her come outside at all."

"And Ben?"

"He's still at Adam's," said Toby.

Libby rushed back outdoors, her mouth very dry, her legs weak. Where had the papers gone?

Vera hurried to her side. "What did you find out?"

Libby told her in a tight voice.

Vera's cheeks and the tip of her nose were red and she shivered. "The book must be here, Libby. If the wind blew it, it would be around here. I didn't see anything but a few leaves and one of Toby's school papers."

"I'll look again!" Libby dashed madly around the yard, searching here and there. She looked under the lilac bushes and close to the chicken pen. Tears filled her eyes and she blinked hard, hunching her shoulders against the wind. What would Jill do if she lost the book? Libby groaned and wrapped her long arms around herself. This had to be one of the very worst days of her entire life!

ELEVEN
Susan

Libby felt sick as she picked up the empty box that once had held Jill's book so securely. What would Jill do now? The book was her dream, her life. Libby moaned and pressed the box to her chest. How could she tell Jill that the book was gone? How could she admit that she'd been careless with the precious pages? She had promised to take care of them!

Slowly Libby walked from her desk to the round red hassock. She sank down with the box on her lap. Jill should have taken the book home with her and none of this would have happened.

At a knock on the door, Libby leaped up, her heart racing. Was it Jill? Frantically Libby shoved the empty box under her bed, then tried to steady her legs as she walked to the door. She sagged in relief to see Vera standing there. She was dressed in faded jeans, a flowered blouse, and a vest that matched the jeans.

"Did you find the book, Libby?"

"No," whispered Libby, her head down.

Vera patted Libby's arm, then walked to the chair

beside the desk and sat down. She smiled at Libby and Libby wondered what there was to smile about as she sank down on the edge of her bed.

Vera crossed her long legs and leaned forward. "Libby, we forgot to pray about this. We've been learning to put God first in our lives, haven't we?"

Libby nodded.

"You and I will pray, agreeing together that we'll find Jill's book. And once we do pray, then we can't worry and fret about it. We must believe that our heavenly Father hears us and will answer us. We have to trust him completely."

Libby remembered other times that God had answered her prayers and she knew he would again. The heavy weight inside seemed to lift and she felt hope rise. As she bowed her head and listened to Vera pray, Libby knew God would answer. He loved her. He wanted to meet her every need, her every care. She lifted her head and smiled, a smile that started deep inside.

"That's my Libby," said Vera, going to her and kissing her warm cheek. "I like to see you happy and not sad and worried."

"Thank you for praying with me, Mom."

"I should have thought of it a while ago." She grinned. "But I'm learning right along with you, Libby. We're all learning more about Jesus and learning to be like him."

"I'm glad," Libby said softly. Sometimes it was hard to realize that Libby Dobbs could talk about Jesus and God without using the names as swear words. But she was Libby Dobbs, a new creature in Christ, and she

didn't swear now. And she was trying to be like Jesus and love like him.

"Would you like to help make supper, Libby?"

Libby nodded. She liked to cook. "I'll be down in a few minutes." She stood at the door and watched Vera walk down the carpeted hall to the stairs. Libby smiled, thankful that Vera was her mom. Soon she'd be really and truly her mom. Marie Dobbs would fade into the past and never have to be called Mother again.

Libby frowned thoughtfully at Susan's closed door. Suddenly the door opened again and Susan stepped out. She stood with her chin high and her fists doubled at her sides.

"What are you looking at?" she asked coldly.

"Did you see Jill's book?"

Susan shrugged. "What if I did?"

"It's gone and I promised to take good care of it." Libby licked her dry lips. "Did you take it, Susan, to get even with me for not calling you to talk on the phone with Joe?"

Susan walked toward Libby and Libby could see the sparks shooting from Susan's blue eyes. "You're not the only one who can get even for things, Libby! And I'm not done yet!"

Libby gasped, her hand fluttering at her throat. "What did you do with Jill's book?"

"Wouldn't you like to know?"

Libby grabbed for Susan, but she dodged and ran. Libby's legs were longer and she caught Susan before she reached the steps. "What did you do with that book? Tell me right now, Susan! You'll be sorry if you don't!"

"You'll never get it back," hissed Susan, twisting and jerking to get away. "Let me go! You're hurting me!"

Libby's grip tightened and Susan cried out. "You'd better tell me, Susan, or I'll break your arm."

"You would, too, wouldn't you? You're good at fighting and hurting people and getting even."

"Shut up!"

"I hate you, Libby! I hate you more than I've ever hated anyone in my life!" Susan twisted and broke free, then dashed down the stairs with Libby following.

Libby felt hot, then cold, as she leaped down the last two steps and grabbed Susan again, almost knocking her into the grandfather clock. "You tell me right now, Susan! Where is that book?"

Susan looked up into Libby's face. "I burned it! I burned it and you're never getting it back!"

Libby dropped her hands to her sides and sank down on the steps. "Oh, Susan!" she whispered in agony. "How could you?"

Susan shrugged. Her hair was mussed and her face hot. Slowly she walked past Libby and back up the stairs.

The tock-tock of the clock seemed to echo inside Libby's head as she sat beside it, her trembling hands over her face.

How could she tell Jill? How could Susan be so mean?

Sounds of laughter from the TV seemed out of place to Libby. What should she do now? How could she ever tell Jill her book was gone forever? Finally she lifted her pale face and pushed herself up.

Slowly she walked to the study and to the phone on Chuck's large oak desk. She would have to tell Jill. That would be the end of her friendship. Jill would hate her as much as Susan did. Maybe more.

Awkwardly Libby dialed Jill's number, then hung up in relief after seven rings. Jill wasn't home yet. Maybe she wouldn't be home until late.

Libby leaned back in Chuck's chair and closed her

eyes. This time God had not answered. Did that mean he didn't care? Her face puckered and a sob escaped. He did care! He did! The Bible said so and Chuck said to believe the Bible no matter what the circumstances.

Suddenly the phone rang and Libby jumped. She answered it.

"Libby, it's Joe."

Joe! Libby's heart raced. "Yes, Joe."

"Could I talk to Susan?"

Libby's hand tightened on the receiver. "She's outside and doesn't want to come in. I think she's playing with Adam." The lies burned in her throat.

"Libby, please call her. I want to talk to her. I promised that I'd call her. I can't stay on the phone too long. Please get Susan for me, Libby."

"Why don't you just talk to me?"

"Why are you doing this? You don't have time for me, Libby. You only have time for your piano."

She bit her lower lip. Why didn't she get Susan for him? "You're the one who doesn't have time for me, Joe. All you ever do is kiss Susan."

"Why are you doing this, Libby? I thought you were different than when you first came to the Johnsons."

"I *am* different!" Then why was she acting the same? Could she be mean to Susan to get even? Susan had burned Jill's book to get even. When would it stop? Libby took a deep breath. "Hang on, Joe. I'll call Susan. She isn't outdoors with Adam or anyone else. She's upstairs in her room."

"Thanks, Libby. Uh . . . Libby."

"Yes?"

"I . . . uh . . . oh, never mind. Get Susan."

Libby frowned thoughtfully as she called upstairs to Susan. She heard Susan rush into Chuck and Vera's bedroom to the extension there, then Libby slowly walked to the study and hung up the phone. She leaned against the desk, her arms folded tightly against herself. Finally she'd done something right. But it was too late to help Jill. How could she rewrite all those pages? Would she even try? Maybe she'd give up her dream.

Libby walked away from the desk and looked out the window at the late afternoon sky. Occasional flakes of snow fell to the ground. Libby closed her eyes and pressed her forehead against the cool pane. "Heavenly Father, forgive me for lying to Joe and for fighting with Susan. I am sorry. I do want to be the new Libby, the Libby you created me to be. Help Susan to forgive me and help me to forgive myself."

She walked to the couch, sat down, and looked around the study. She remembered the many times she'd been called in there to talk to Chuck. Now most of the talks were about school, but before he'd had to scold her and tell her how to act. In this very room she'd accepted Jesus as her personal Savior. Tears filled her eyes. She would never, never forget that day.

Libby turned her head at a sound at the door. Susan stood there, her face pale, tears in her eyes and on her cheeks. Libby pushed herself up and stood facing Susan.

"Why did you do that?" whispered Susan, clenching and unclenching her hands.

"Do what?" Libby thought she meant keep the phone from her for so long.

"Why did you call me for Joe's call?"

Libby shrugged. It was too hard to put her thoughts into words.

"Oh, Libby!" wailed Susan, then turned and ran away.

Libby stood very still. What had she done wrong this time?

TWELVE
Never give up a dream

Libby peeked around two boys at Jill. She seemed to be listening to Connie Tol's Sunday school lesson. Libby looked down at the Bible in her hands. She couldn't keep her mind on anything but how angry Jill had been when she'd told her about the book.

"But how could you let it out of your sight?" Jill had screamed over the phone early this morning.

"I don't know."

"You never did think it was important, did you?"

"Yes, I did." But Libby knew she hadn't thought it was as important as her piano had been.

"I won't be best friends with you, Libby Dobbs. I won't be friends with you at all!"

And she'd slammed down the receiver and Libby had gone back to her room and sobbed against her pillow until she'd had to do morning chores. Breakfast had stuck in her throat. She had snapped at Susan when she'd tried to talk to her. Chuck and Vera had both asked her what was wrong but she couldn't bring herself to tell them.

By the time class was over Libby's head ached and she wanted to go home and crawl into bed and bury herself under the covers. During church she sang the songs and sat very quietly while the pastor spoke, but she didn't hear what he said. Jill sat three rows ahead with her parents and she didn't glance back once.

At dinner Vera asked her if she was feeling ill and Chuck said he wanted to see her in his study right after the table was cleared. Today was the boys' day to do dishes but she and Susan had to help clean off the table.

Libby refused the chocolate pie for dessert, knowing it would stick in her throat. Was Chuck going to scold her for something? She peeked at him but he was laughing and talking to Kevin and he didn't look stern at all. His tie was loosened and his jacket hung over the back of his chair. His sleeves were rolled part way up on his tanned arms.

"Libby, I want to talk to you," said Susan in a very low voice.

Libby frowned and shook her head. What could Susan want now? It sure wouldn't be to apologize.

Several minutes later Libby walked hesitantly into the study. Chuck turned from the window and walked toward her, his hazel eyes troubled.

"Elizabeth, let's sit down and talk, shall we?"

She sat down, her heart racing.

"Relax, honey. I'm not going to scold you."

She locked her fingers together, her eyes hard on him. What did he want?

"Honey, whatever is going on between you and Susan must be resolved. It's put the entire household into an uproar. I want you and Susan to sit down together and talk."

Libby twisted her toe on the carpet and looked down at her locked fingers. Had Susan told him that she'd burned Jill's book?

"I talked to Susan this morning, but got nowhere with her. She said she'd try to talk to you. Will you try also, Elizabeth?"

She took a deep breath and nodded slightly.

"Just remember that God is with you both. He wants the best for both of you."

Just then someone knocked and Chuck called out to come in. Susan walked in, her face pale, her eyes large.

"I need to talk to Libby right now, Dad," she said in a hoarse whisper. "Alone, OK?"

Chuck stood up and Libby wanted to run from the room with him. He touched Susan's cheek. "Remember your heavenly Father is helping you, honey."

She nodded and Libby thought she would faint.

Susan sank down on a chair facing Libby. "I . . . I am sorry, Libby. I've been mean to you. Forgive me, please."

Libby blinked in surprise. She managed to nod and whisper that she wanted Susan to forgive her.

Susan pushed her red-gold hair back with a shaking hand. "Libby, I have to tell you about Jill's book."

"What's to tell? It's too late now, Susan. It's just too late." Libby leaned back and tried to push away from her thoughts the terrible look on Jill's face.

"No," whispered Susan, then said louder. "No!"

"But it is!"

"Libby, I didn't burn the book. I just said I did to hurt

you. I didn't think you'd tell Jill. I didn't want to hurt her. I'm sorry. I am *so* sorry! I saw the papers on the picnic table and I knew that you and Jill had been reading them and so I took them. I was going to give them back as soon as I made you really sorry for not telling me about Joe's phone call. I couldn't. I was afraid of what you would do. And then I tried to tell you this morning and you wouldn't let me." She held out her hands. "I am sorry."

Libby shook her head, unable to speak. Susan had Jill's book! She had not burned it after all.

"Say something, Libby."

Libby cleared her throat and tried to speak, but couldn't.

"I didn't know you'd tell Jill so soon." Susan jumped up and paced the floor. Finally she turned back to Libby. "I'll tell Jill if that will make it better for you."

"No. I'll tell her." She pushed her fingers through her hair. "I'll tell her."

Susan sat down again and leaned forward. "Libby."

"Yes?"

"I'll give up Joe if you want me to. I really will."

"Good. You don't need him."

"I love him."

"But you aren't the same now that you love Joe," snapped Libby.

"I felt bad about Joe because I knew you liked him, Libby. I didn't want him for a boyfriend when I thought you loved him, but I couldn't help myself."

Libby rubbed her hand down her jeans. "I . . . I don't like Joe that way. Honest I don't." And she didn't! "If you want to, that's all right with me. I . . . I guess I was wrong about that."

Susan's face brightened. "Are you sure?"

Libby nodded.

"And you forgive me?" asked Susan breathlessly.

Libby nodded with a slight smile. She was glad for the happy look on Susan's face. "And you forgive me?"

"Oh, yes!" Susan bobbed up and threw her arms around Libby, hugging her hard. Libby hugged her back, a laugh bubbling up.

"I'll leave so you can call Jill and talk to her," said Susan, walking toward the door. She pulled open the door and Jill stood there, her hand raised to knock. She looked gigantic next to Susan.

"Come in," said Susan weakly. "I'll let you girls talk alone." She closed the door behind her and Libby stood looking up at Jill and wondered about the strange look on Jill's face.

"Hi, Libby." Jill tugged her sweater closer around herself.

"Hi. I . . . I have something to say."

Jill held out her hand. "Wait. Please, let me talk first. I'm very sorry for being angry with you. I don't want us to stop being best friends. I had a long talk with Dad a while ago. He made me realize that when a setback comes, you can't give up. I will rewrite my book and I'll write it better than before. Dad said never to give up a dream. Just because I lost a book doesn't mean I can just quit writing. I will make it yet, Libby! I sure will!"

Never give up a dream! The words rang through Libby's head. That's exactly what she'd done. She had given up her dream and she should not have! But it was different with Jill. Jill's book was not destroyed. She would not have to start all over. But she hadn't known that. Libby moved restlessly. Jill had been determined to start over. Libby took a deep breath. Should she start over too?

"What's wrong, Libby?"

Libby laughed breathlessly. "Nothing. Will you let me talk now?"

Jill shrugged. "Sure. What do you want to say?"

"Let's find Susan first. She has something important to say to you."

"Susan does?" Jill frowned thoughtfully. "I didn't think Susan even liked me. She acts like being big is a disease."

Libby chuckled and Jill joined in as they walked out of the study and upstairs.

Susan opened her door at the first knock. "Come in. Did you tell her, Libby?"

"No."

"Tell me what?"

Susan walked to her desk and opened the top drawer. She pulled out a sheaf of papers and held them out to Jill. Libby watched Jill's face and saw the disbelief, then surprise, then joy.

Quietly Susan told what she'd done, then apologized to Jill.

Jill looked over the pages, then held them to her, then looked them over again. Tears ran down her cheeks and she rubbed them quickly again.

Libby blinked away tears in her eyes and she saw Susan do the same.

"My book," said Jill again and again. Then she looked up sharply at Susan. "Did you read it?"

Susan hesitated, then nodded slowly.

"Susan reads a lot," said Libby quickly. "She could

probably tell you if it's as good as other books."

"I liked it, Jill," said Susan brightly. "I really did. I want to know how it's going to end."

Jill looked down, then at Susan. "I'll let you read it when I'm done if you want."

Libby looked from her best friend to her sister. They had solved their problems. Now, it was her turn. But hadn't she already made the only decision possible? She was a failure at piano.

Piano!

Libby grabbed Susan's arm. "Now, can you tell me what you did with my tiny piano?"

Susan sighed unhappily. "Libby, I didn't take it. Honest."

Libby dropped her hand. She believed Susan this time. Since Susan hadn't take the piano, who had?

THIRTEEN
The mystery solved

Libby watched Susan walk across her bedroom to answer the knock at the door. Jill sat on the floor beside Libby.

"Hi, Mom." Susan held the door wide and Vera walked in, smiled at them and sat on the chair at Susan's desk.

"I thought I might get in on the girl talk," said Vera, her blue eyes twinkling.

"We found Jill's book," said Libby, motioning to the papers in Jill's hands.

"I'm glad," said Vera. "I think it's wonderful that you're writing a book, Jill. It must make you feel great."

Jill nodded and Libby knew that she felt self-conscious talking about her book to an adult.

"Did Joe call yet, Mom?" asked Susan anxiously. She twisted a piece of hair around and around her finger.

"Not yet, hon." Vera chuckled. "I remember when I first fell in love."

Libby gasped. Vera in love with someone besides Chuck!

"Don't be shocked, Libby." Vera fingered the gold chain around her neck. "God created men and women to be together. God planned it that way and that's why boys fall in love with girls and girls fall in love with boys. It's always that way."

"Not for me!" cried Libby, lifting her pointed chin.

"Oh, Libby," snapped Susan with a frown. "You don't like anything but piano."

Libby stiffened but kept her mouth closed tightly.

"Libby, the time will come when boys will be important to you," said Vera, shaking her head and smiling. "Some girls start sooner than others. It's a part of growing up."

"Tell us about the boy you first loved," said Jill.

Vera sat with her hands locked around her knee. "His name was Dick Preston and he had brown hair and dark brown eyes. He was fourteen years old and I was twelve. Every time I talked to him I'd practically faint. And when he talked to me I'd feel dizzy for the rest of the day. Once he sat with me at a football game and I thought for sure he'd ask me to marry him."

"Did he kiss you?" whispered Susan, her face red.

"No. But I wanted him to. I didn't get kissed until I was thirteen. The boy's name was Jason Alerding."

"I'm going to love Joe always," said Susan dreamily.

"I've heard of a man and woman who fell in love in elementary school and stayed in love and got married," said Jill. "That would make a very interesting book."

"Not to me," said Libby, wrinkling her nose.

"I'll read it if you write it, Jill," said Susan.

Libby pulled her knees up and rested her chin on them. She didn't want to hear any more of this but she was forced to listen to the others. Didn't they know the conversation was boring? She would not fall in love the way Susan had. Boys were fine as friends, but that was all! And she'd sure never let a boy kiss her. How gross!

Several minutes later she was able to pry Jill away and they walked outdoors together. Jill held the box with her book inside. A cold wind blew color into Libby's cheeks and turned her nose red.

"Libby, listen to me." Jill stopped and something in her voice made Libby's heart jump. "Don't get mad, will you?"

"What is it?"

"Don't give up your dream of being a concert pianist."

"I have to!"

"No, you don't!"

Libby knotted her fists and stuffed them into her jacket pocket. What did Jill know about it, anyway? "I can't play the piano. It's simple. I have to quit. I have to give up my dream."

"Just practice more, Libby. You can't quit because of one failure."

"Let's drop the subject, Jill. I don't want to talk about it anymore. I'm sick of the whole thing."

"You're not a quitter, Libby. Why are you acting like one?"

"Why don't you just go home? First you bore me to death talking about boys and now you lecture me about piano as if you knew what you were talking about." Libby's hazel eyes flashed and she stamped her foot in the damp grass. Jill sure couldn't be her best friend if she was going to make her mad.

Jill pressed her box tightly against herself. “I’m trying to help you, Libby. You sure won’t get help from anyone else since I’m the only one who knows how you’re feeling.”

“And that’s the way it’ll stay!”

“I should tell your parents that you aren’t going to be a concert pianist. They’d sure set you straight.”

Libby’s head felt as if it were being squeezed by a tight band around it. Maybe her brains would pop right out. Then Jill would be sorry for talking about piano when she didn’t want her to.

Jill pulled back her sleeve and looked at her watch. “I’d like to stay and discuss this more but I promised my folks that I’d be home by four. See you on the bus in the morning.” She wrinkled her nose. “School tomorrow. If I didn’t have to go to gym and have all the girls make fun of me, I’d enjoy going to school.”

Libby started to say something unkind, then bit her tongue and refused to say it. “See you in the morning, Jill. I’m glad your book is safe with you.”

“Maybe we can think of a description of the man for Glenda on the bus.”

“Maybe.” But Libby didn’t want to think about it or talk about it. She didn’t want Jill to get so interested in boys that she’d forget her dream to write a book and make it by the time she was sixteen or even fourteen.

Libby walked to the end of the driveway with Jill, then watched as she walked along the road toward home. Two cars and a pickup drove past. Rex barked and Libby wished that she’d untied him so he could be with her now. He always made her feel better.

Just as she turned to go toward the house, she heard

her name called. She turned to find Joe running toward her. For a minute she wanted to dash to the house and not see him or talk to him, but she waited for him. He stopped beside her, panting for breath. His face and ears were red from the cold. His fleece-lined corduroy jacket looked warm.

"Susan's in the house," said Libby.

"I know."

"Did you want to talk to her?"

He nodded with a sharp look at Libby. What on earth was he thinking? Why was he looking at her that way?

"So, go talk to her," snapped Libby. "Don't let me stop you."

He caught her arm and stopped her from running off. "Libby, why are you doing this to me?"

"Me? It's you, Joe. Why are you doing this to me?" She looked down at his hand then up at him. He had grown until he was several inches taller than she was and she'd never noticed before.

"Libby, aren't we friends?"

She stared at him in surprise. "*You* don't want to be friends. All you can think about is kissing Susan or talking to Susan or holding Susan's hand!"

He ducked his head. "I know. But Libby, listen to me. I love Susan. She's my girlfriend. Does that stop us from being friends?"

Libby frowned thoughtfully. "I guess it doesn't, does it? I think I got upset about you and Susan and didn't stop to think that we could still be friends. I thought you hated me because I didn't have time for you."

"And I thought you hated me because of Susan."

Libby grinned sheepishly. "Maybe I did, Joe, but not anymore. I guess if Susan wants you for a boyfriend and not just a friend, I won't care. But not me! I don't want a boyfriend!"

Joe tipped back his head and laughed. "Having a boyfriend is not a disease, Libby."

"But it sure puts everything else out of your mind."

He shrugged. "I guess you're right."

"But Mom says it's part of growing up, so I won't say anything else about it." She grinned, then walked with him up the long driveway.

He stopped her again near the back door. "Libby, I have to give you something."

"You do?" Was it a present?

He reached in his jacket pocket and pulled something out, then held out his hand to her. On his palm sat the tiny piano that he'd given her a long time ago.

"How did you get it?" she asked in a low, tight voice. Had Susan taken it and given it to him?

"I hate to say."

It had been Susan! "Tell me, Joe. I want to know." She held the piano carefully.

"I saw it sitting on the windowsill in your kitchen and I thought you didn't want it anymore because you were mad at me. I decided that I'd take it back. But I've been thinking that that's a lot like stealing and I just couldn't keep it another day. I brought it back to you and if you don't want it, then you can toss it out or give it away or do whatever you want to do with it."

She smiled, blinking back tears. "Joe, I want it. It was sitting on the windowsill because Mom had to fix a broken leg on it."

"Oh, Libby. I'm sorry for taking it."

"That's OK, Joe. I'm glad to have it back." She couldn't wait to show it to Susan.

"Piano is your life, Libby. I was mad about that for a while, but I can understand now. It is important for you to spend time practicing. You have a talent and you have to use it. Grandma Feuder told me. She said when God gives you a talent, you must use it or you'll lose it."

Libby shivered. She didn't want to lose her talent for piano, did she? God had given her the talent to play, but what was she doing with it? Throwing it away, that's what!

"You look funny, Libby. Don't you feel good?"

She cleared her throat. "I'm OK."

"I want to go in and see Susan now. I told her I'd be right over." He smiled. "I missed her while I was at Grandma's."

"Oh, Joe. You're silly."

He ducked his head and grinned. "I know. I can't help it."

Libby pulled open the back door. "Let's get inside so you can see Susan before your heart breaks with loneliness."

Joe hung his jacket beside Susan's red one. He touched her jacket and Libby rolled her eyes in disgust.

"Joe."

He turned to her, his eyebrows raised questioningly.

"Thanks for bringing back my tiny piano."

"That's all right."

They smiled at each other and she knew she had her friend again. He walked toward the family room and she looked down at the piano in her hand. This piano would always be silent, but did the piano in the family room have to be? Maybe she could play just for her own enjoyment even if she would never be a famous concert pianist.

"I will," she whispered in determination. She'd play just for fun, just enough to keep her talent.

FOURTEEN
The future concert pianist

Libby opened the song book and set it in place on the piano. She squirmed on the bench until she was sitting comfortably. Shivers of excitement ran up and down her spine. Oh it was good to be back at the piano!

She touched the keys lovingly, saying hello to them after being gone for more than a week. She was glad that Joe and Susan had gone to the basement. Kevin and Toby were upstairs and Ben was at Adam's, playing chess again.

A fire crackled in the fireplace, then the sound was covered by the music coming from the piano, made by piano fingers. Libby smiled as she played. Oh, she was playing again! She didn't want to stop.

At the end of the second piece, clapping startled Libby. She looked over her should to find Vera and Chuck standing, listening to her.

"That was beautiful, Libby," said Vera, nodding and smiling. "You have a very special talent, honey."

"You are going to be the most famous concert pianist around," said Chuck proudly. "I know you are."

Libby leaped up, her heart racing. "No! I won't be! I

should have told you before." She locked and unlocked her fingers, hurting them.

"Settle down, Elizabeth." Chuck squeezed her thin shoulder and she forced herself to calm down.

She looked from Chuck to Vera. "I know that you're paying a lot of money to Rachael Avery for piano lessons. But I won't need them anymore. I'm not good enough to be a concert pianist. I'm not going to be one."

"Let's sit down," said Vera softly. She sat on the couch and Chuck joined her. Libby sat cross-legged on the floor with her back against the piano bench.

"I won't change my mind," said Libby firmly.

"Let's talk about it, Elizabeth," said Chuck just as firmly. "We all know you have talent."

"But not enough!" cried Libby, gripping her knees tightly with her hands. "You know that and I know that!"

"Why do you say that, honey?" asked Vera.

"I am a failure, Mom. You heard me at the recital. I couldn't play. I made too many mistakes after I was finally able to play. I was so, *so* embarrassed!"

Chuck clicked his tongue. "Never give up a dream because of one little failure."

"Little failure?" Libby couldn't believe what she was hearing.

"That's right. Little failure. You did very well for your first time in front of an audience. The next time will be easier and better."

Libby jumped up, her fists doubled. "Didn't you hear me? There will never be a next time! I will not make a fool of myself again!"

"Libby, sit down for just a few minutes." Vera stood

up and walked to the stereo. "I want you to listen to something."

Reluctantly Libby sat back on the floor and watched Vera. Soon piano music exploded from the record that Vera had put on the stereo. Libby listened as the music enveloped her. Oh, if only she could play like that!

Finally the piano music stopped and Libby wanted to hear it over and over.

"Libby, that was Sarah Neeley. Today she is famous. I read an article about her just a few weeks ago. She said that she almost stopped studying piano when she was younger because she fumbled through several recitals. Her teachers were ready to give up on her, but she had a dream and she was willing to work for that dream. She decided that she would play and she would play well. She refused to think of failure, and look where she is today. You heard the music that comes from her fingers. Libby, you have that music in you. I know you do and you know you do. One failure should not put you down."

Chuck slipped his arm around Vera. "Mom is right, Elizabeth. You can't stop because of an embarrassment. Allow God to take away that bad feeling and give you a feeling of security and accomplishment."

Libby looked at her fingers and felt the piano bench against her back. Was she willing to give up now? Suddenly the idea seemed terrible to her. She couldn't give up her dream any more than she could give up breathing. It was a part of her, given to her by God himself.

"I can see by that smile that you are ready to get in there and start working again," said Chuck with a wide grin. "That's our Elizabeth!"

"Play for us, honey," said Vera.

Libby hesitated and Vera urged her on. Finally Libby sat at the piano, her fingers on the keys.

Chuck stood behind her and rested his hands on her shoulders. "Honey, we're prayed for you often and God is answering. Embarrassment will not hinder you again. You will play with confidence because God is with you."

Libby smiled up at him. "Thanks, Dad. I will always remember that." And she knew she would. She knew the next time she had to walk in front of a crowd of people to perform for them, she'd walk in confidence because God would be with her and she wouldn't forget. She'd play to her heavenly Father as well as the audience. As she touched the first notes she thanked God for the talent he'd given her and she promised that she would use that talent the way he wanted her to.

Music filled the room—her music—and she wanted to sing and shout. She played her recital song again and she played it without error. When she finished she turned, then flushed red. All of her family as well as Joe were sitting listening to her. They clapped and Toby cheered. Slowly she stood up and bowed.

She would not give up her dream!

The next morning she waited excitedly for Jill to get on the school bus. She couldn't wait to tell her best friend her decision.

Jill hesitated just inside the bus and Libby wildly motioned to her to come back. The younger boys and girls were extra noisy as they shouted that it was snowing, really snowing. Libby knew Ben would be glad. Now he and Adam would have more to do than play chess.

Jill sat down and slumped low in the seat beside Libby. "I didn't know if you'd still be mad or not, Libby."

"I'm not mad, Jill. I'm happy."

Jill sat up straight and turned to stare down at Libby. "You are happy! What happened? Hurry, tell me!"

So Libby did and Jill beamed.

"That's the best news I've heard in a long time, Libby. Now, tell me how it feels to be the future famous concert pianist, Elizabeth Gail Johnson?"

"It feels . . ." Libby searched for the right word. "It feels absolutely fantastic!"

Jill held out a piece of paper. "Can I have your autograph?"

Libby laughed. "If I can have yours." Suddenly the smile left Libby's face. "I just thought of Joanne Tripper. She was prepared to step in my place with Rachael Avery. Joanne doesn't know how close she came to doing just that."

"Will you tell her?"

Libby settled back in her seat with a chuckle. "Are you kidding? I will tell her that she can't stop me from being famous. If she'll let me, I'll tell her to quit working so hard to get me away from Rachael Avery and work at playing the piano. Who knows? Maybe Joanne Tripper will be a famous concert pianist too."

"Maybe so, Libby."

The bus stopped at the school and Libby pushed her way out of the bus. Today was a perfect day. She lifted her face to the falling snow and silently thanked her heavenly Father for the day and for her talent.

Jill nudged Libby. "How does it feel to be short and thin and happy, with snow falling on you?"

Libby laughed as Jill stood beside her, a pencil poised over a piece of paper. "It feels short and thin and happy and wet."